A Peculiar Magic

A Peculiar Magic

ANNABEL and EDGAR JOHNSON

Illustrated by Lynd Ward

HOUGHTON MIFFLIN COMPANY BOSTON / 1965

CONTENTS

To J. S. B.

A Peculiar Magic

I

The Supe

I

THERE WAS A SOUND of anger in the air — a riot sound that charged the hot night. Cindy started up out of a restless sleep. In the darkness, she listened as the noise broke out nearer, along the next block. Men shouting — like another posse on the hunt! Spilling out of bed, she hurried to the window.

Beyond the close little room a wind was astir, heavy with the smell of dust and leather and cattle. Big herds were coming in every day now. Over in the corrals by the railroad tracks they were bawling, as if they too had sensed trouble. From out along the street came the clatter of hooves, galloping . . . and uptown a burst of gunfire.

Of course that might not mean anything except a

few cowpokes letting off steam — swaggering, bearded galoots just in off a long drive and itching for fun. It made Cindy wince, to think of them crowding into the dance hall, the stomp and click of feet going on until daybreak. Her mother would come home so tired she could hardly walk.

"I didn't sit out a single dance," she would say, after a big night like this, trying to sound gay about it. Then she would take Cindy in her arms with that wonderful, rich love. "Never mind, dearest. Don't hate it so. Oh, it's a curious way to make a living, I know. But this is Kansas, and you have to learn to take new places as you find them. I'm lucky to have a job, and just think, we've got enough to pay the back rent and buy groceries until the end of the month."

Always just barely enough. Cindy's hands clenched helplessly at her sides. Whenever she thought about her mother being pumped around the floor by those grinning trail drivers, she just about choked. The room seemed to get narrower and hotter, she had to get away. Right now, she wished she could find out what that noise was about.

Stripping off her nightgown she went to rummage in the box under the bed, digging out her rough clothes — denim shirt and dungarees. She hauled them on fast, pulled on her walking boots. They were scuffed from roaming out along the edge of the prairie and up and down the back alleys of the seedy little town. Small and wirey as she was, she could pass for a boy in the

4

dark. Most people never gave her a second glance. Except the sheriff.

As she pinned the dark braids tight to her head and plunked the old straw hat down low over her eyes, Cindy was thinking about that. It couldn't be pure chance, the way he seemed to appear lately whenever she felt like slipping out at night. Over by the corrals, or just up the street — there he'd be. She knew he had it in for her, because along with being sheriff he was truant officer, too. More than once last spring he had caught her playing hookey. But school was out now. None of his business where she went.

So far she'd always seen him in time to duck, but Cindy thought she'd better keep a sharp lookout tonight. Quietly she opened the door and scouted the hallway. The old house felt empty. Most of the roomers were dance-hall girls, off at work now. Cindy headed for the rear stairs; at the bottom she set the door ajar and stood a minute scanning the corrals and sheds out in back. The uproar seemed to be coming from the railroad yards now. From beyond the row of stables — hoarse voices and the slanting, shifting light of flares.

Someone was coming from over there — a man, running. As he came past she called softly, "What's up?"

"Another raid!" He swore as he ran on. "Fellows ain't gonna like this . . ."

Nobody liked it — the way the Ladies' Reform Society was trying to turn the town proper. A bunch of fussy-looking women in dark clothes and lace under their chins, pestering the mayor to pass laws, charging into the sheriff's office, making him nervous. They'd forced him to close down all the places that served "spiritous refreshment," as they called it. Heaven only knew what they were up to, now!

Cindy could hear the sheriff's booming voice, bellowing orders, but the words were lost in the shrill of a train whistle. The Denver Express — but it wasn't thundering straight on through as usual. Slowing down now, engine spitting red coals, it rolled through the yards, its big white eye of a headlight piercing the night — came to a hissing stop.

Just like last week! When they'd rounded up all the gamblers, flagged down the Express and hustled them aboard for a one-way ride out of town! Cindy slipped out into the darkness and headed for the yards. In the hubbub over beyond the stables she caught the high pitch of women's voices, and began to run. No! no! no! the words pounded in her with every step. They'd never pick on the dance hall — her mother had been so sure of that!

"It's the only decent place the boys can go for a little pleasure," she'd said. "Nobody could pass a law against anything as harmless as dancing." But Cindy had her own ideas about that. From what she'd seen of people they could make any rules they wanted to.

She was skirting the long dark row of horse barns when a couple of men rounded the corner, carrying flares. Quickly she ducked into the open stable door as they came toward her.

". . . a bad business if you ask me," one was saying. "I ain't signing on again for deputy, not if it means hustling women around. Those hurdy-gurdy gals wasn't bothering nobody."

"Aw, you know them lady reformers . . . see folks havin' too much fun, they get all scandalized . . ."

As they went on past, Cindy held still, clenched up so hard she could scarcely breathe. Out beyond the barns she could hear the train pulling out, chuffing slowly, then faster and faster. With her nerves a-tremble she made herself stand frozen. But inside she was crying out — *not Mother!* They couldn't have sent her away, too. She'd have told them she had a daughter — nobody could be that terrible! They must have let her stay. *I've got to find out!*

But there were more men coming this way now. Striding along in the light of the flares, the sheriff was in the lead, grumbling, ". . . not exactly to my taste, either, boys, but we've got to finish the job. Try to be kind to the young'un when you pick her up. She's in for a shock. But watch out you don't lose her, she can cover ground like a jackrabbit."

". . . can't go far in this town."

"All the same, I don't want any slip-ups," the sheriff snapped. "These reformin' females . . . got their umbrellas swingin' . . . Blamin me — as if I got time to

7

watch out for every little tomboy that skins over a fence. Well, it'll be their job now."

One of the deputies mumbled a question and the sheriff snorted.

"I'm glad I don't have to decide. There's a half-dozen of them ladies hankerin' to take charge of the little gal — no, that's up to the Judge. 'Long as they keep her out of mischief, that's all I ask. You boys take the front, I'll go up the back way . . ."

As the men strode on off toward the rooming house, Cindy tried to grasp it — that it was her they were talking about. The Reform Society, making some kind of plans — with the Judge! She was going to be given away to one of those ladies?

What about Mother! And even as the question leaped up, Cindy knew the answer — that Jill Ferris had been put on that train, too. Just another dance-hall girl whose feelings don't count. What did they care, those priss-mouthed people with their whispers? ". . . a sin and a shame, for a woman with a child . . . to take such kind of work." Oh, Cindy had heard them and despised them. Now she could have grappled with them and kicked and bit and fought, in her fury. But there were too many — with the Judge to back them up! "Discipline . . . that's what a twelve-year-old girl needs . . ." She'd heard their little sniffings about "the welfare of the child." And right now, sending the posse after her. She had to think fast — how to save herself.

Over in the old frame building she had just left, she could see the torches moving as the deputies searched the rooms. They'd be out again any minute — hunting her. Instinctively she shrank back deeper into the pitch-black of the barn, groping along the stalls where the horses stood shuffling and snorting softly as she stole past. A good thing she knew every inch of these stables. There was a small door at the far end near the tracks. And across the railroad yards was open prairie. If she could just lay low there, long enough to think — to steady herself and try to figure what to do —

But now she heard a movement behind her! A man had come in at the door of the stable, dodged in fast, but silently. She'd just caught a quick glimpse of the shadowy figure and then he was here in the dark with her. Coming this way, walking almost noiselessly. Cindy hurried to reach the rear door, but in her rush she stumbled and went down on all fours. As she scrambled up, a hand caught her, powerful fingers gripping her arm.

"Hold, on, friend, let's take a look at you." The quiet voice had a dangerous edge on it. He struck a match, and in the brief flare of light, she knew him. The piano player at the dance hall. She'd seen him, those nights when she'd sneaked over to look in through the rear windows — a dark, moody figure sitting on his raised platform, raking off fast music. And always on the watch, as if he was searching —or being hunted.

Now, so close to him, she could see a swift alertness in his eyes. In the matchlight they seemed to burn blue-white for an instant, as if he recognized her, too.

"Another fugitive from justice." He pinched out the flame and released her. "No need to worry that you'll be yelling for the sheriff." As he went on past to the narrow doorway, he made a long, lean silhouette against the moving lights out there in the railroad yards. When she tried to slip past, he nudged her back. "Still too many deputies around."

In the glow from the flares, she could see his face set in a hard, controlled kind of anger. For all that his clothes had a handsome quality, there was a toughness about the straight line of his mouth, the way he held himself — light and ready. Even though she knew this was no man to take any chances with, Cindy fairly ached to ask him a few questions.

"What did happen?" she burst out in a hushed voice, dreading to hear. "Did they — they didn't put *everybody* on that train!"

"With one exception. I suppose they didn't figure a musician could give them much trouble." He glanced down at his hand. In the ruddy light she could see that the knuckles were bloody. "They were more concerned about some of the women — especially your mother. Took three deputies to escort her aboard."

"How do you know who I am?" she demanded, instantly leery.

"You're more famous than you think." There was a

10

faint mockery in his words. "The Judge seemed to have a whole bill of particulars on the activities of Lucinda Ferris. He went into considerable detail with your mother as to how she'd failed to bring you up properly. I wasn't paying too much attention — I was sizing up my own opportunities." As he spoke in that low voice he was scanning the railroad yards.

Cindy shuddered as she thought of the scene — how it must have been with her mother arguing, finally struggling with them. In a rush she said, "They'll never get me — I'll hide! I'll find some place — "

"Hiding's too temporary to suit me." The man's voice was level and calculating. "Some situations call for a complete departure. And I think my transportation is getting the steam up." He was watching a train of empty cattle cars on a siding nearby. It must have pulled off the main track just to let the Express go through, for now the engine was beginning to pour forth thick smoke.

And headed in the right direction — toward Denver! Cindy seized on the idea. In a minute that train would be busting along just a few miles behind the Express. And it made sense to get out of this place fast. Just leave it all behind. Nothing to stay here for, nothing but to be seized and bound over to somebody for discipline and rules, locked up at nights. Or maybe all the time . . .

The lights were closing in around the lower end of the stables now, deputies coming this way — looking

11

for her. Cindy forgot the man, forgot everything but the need to escape. Darting out into the yards, she ran for the train. It let out a long shriek of the whistle, a shudder broke along the string of cars and they began to roll.

She raced for the nearest one with an open door, but it was too high off the ground. She'd never make it! And then strong hands caught her up and chucked her inside like a sack of potatoes. The piano player swung himself into the car with the light agility of a cat. And they were safe. It had happened so fast, no one had even seen them.

So fast — that only now Cindy felt a sudden twinge of doubt. She hadn't really meant to have anything to do with this man. Yet here she was, rattling along with him through the night. And not even sure where they were going.

2

As Cindy watched the last lights of town slip away into the darkness, it gave her an empty, lost kind of feeling. Even though she knew she was lucky to be free, it was a vast, trackless country all around. Far behind to the east, a three-quarter moon was spreading a pale brilliance across the endless prairies. How many hundreds of miles of them, stretching away?

The train was picking up speed now, the rickety car clattering and swaying along. Cindy stood, hanging onto the slats, staring out into the night, but sharply aware of the man behind her. She tried to remember what she had heard about him.

Durango, they called him — nobody knew where he'd come from or the rest of his name, if that was his real name. They said he'd just walked into the dance hall one night out of nowhere and asked for a job. Most people suspected he was in some trouble and was running from the law. But when the manager heard him play, he was hired — no questions asked.

Something disturbing about his music — the girls said there were times when it sounded as if the Devil had got into his fingers. But whenever they'd start to gossip about him, her mother would make them hush. "It's not right to talk of others behind their backs," she'd say, but Cindy had a hunch it was more than that. As if Jill Ferris had some suspicions of her own about this man. Something Cindy wasn't supposed to hear. She shivered slightly.

"Lend you my coat," he offered.

"No, thank you." She didn't like to think he was watching her so closely. She could almost feel him — figuring something as he sat there in the loose straw at the front end of the car where he had made himself comfortable. She bet he'd been in plenty of jams like this, to take it so easy. But he'd never bargained to have a girl tagging along, so he must be planning something right now.

Cindy knew she ought to be trying to make some plan, herself. But all at once, with the cool wind off the plains whipping in her face she was beginning to feel the full chill of everything — all that had happened. The truth kept getting more real, like a deep cut when it starts to hurt. She went over it and over it — the

14

dance hall raided, her mother sent away, and the Judge and sheriff going to decide her whole fate.

"The dirty buzzards!" She must have said it aloud for Durango made a short sound like a snort of derision.

"Seemed to me they were quite considerate to provide such first-class accommodations for the girls."

"If you thought it was so wonderful, why didn't you go along with them?" It came out pretty uppity, but it helped Cindy to keep from faltering inside. Something about that confidence of his was making her uneasy.

"Always did prefer to travel at my own convenience," he said.

"Anyhow, why didn't you try to help the rest, once you did get away from the posse? You could've got the drop on them and — "

"Never carry a gun," Durango said carelessly. "Gets a man in trouble. And there's not much opportunity in jail — especially for a musician."

"Well, you could've set fire to something and while everybody was putting it out, you — you could've got the cowboys all riled, and they'd mob the sheriff." Even if it wasn't sensible, Cindy had to let loose in some direction.

Durango seemed amused. "The Reform Society would have had an interesting time, trying to tame you."

"Those nosey old biddies, why didn't they mind their own business?" she stormed angrily. "It's a free country — I've got a right to go where I please and do what I have to!"

"Such as roaming the streets at night in boys' clothes? Great balls of fire, girl, didn't your mother ever mention the hazards of such behavior?"

"Don't you blame her!" Cindy retorted. "She always tells me to stay home and be patient. Only sometimes I can't! And these clothes she doesn't even know about. I traded them from a boy for some spurs I had, and a lariat, and I traded those off another boy for a baby badger I found that the landlord wouldn't let me keep. *So it's not Mother's fault!*"

"Was she also unaware that you skipped school? The Judge was especially upset about that."

"She was asleep. She didn't know where I was!" Cindy retorted. "And after the sheriff came around and told her, and she said I mustn't do it any more, then I didn't — not so much anyhow. Only it's so boring, all that arithmetic and memorizing poems and the imports and the exports — if I don't feel like all that, who cares? Who cares what I do?"

"A number of people seem to have taken an interest," he said with a short laugh, "enough to get you in trouble. And your mother, too, of course. She must be nearly out of her mind, worrying right now."

"Don't talk about that!" Cindy yelled.

For the first time, Durango seemed irritated. "No need to shout. You must've got your tongue from your father's side of the family."

"I don't have a father! He was killed in the war."

And she certainly wasn't going to tell how he had deserted them first, when she was just a little baby. And that he wasn't a hero, either, not even a soldier. He'd got shot while he was running the blockade, to make money — Cindy didn't understand it all. Her mother had never said a bad word about him. What she'd learned she had picked up from Grandma and the other people back in Missouri in the town where Cindy had grown up. "Anyhow, that's why my mother has to work so hard, and so don't you say anything against her."

"No, I'm beginning to see you've made your own bed," he remarked dryly. "All the same, it was probably a mistake, to bring you to a rowdy cow town — "

"We couldn't help that, either," Cindy flared out. "After the South lost the war, we didn't have any money. And then there was a depression and the mill closed, Mother couldn't get another job. It wasn't anybody's fault, it was *people*."

Durango seemed to consider that a minute. "People — yes. I'd say you're right, there — people are certainly the cause of most of our nuisance." The amused way he turned the words back on her made Cindy boil. Oh, she knew what he meant, that she was the nuisance right now — to him.

"Don't worry," she said. "I won't be a bother to you. Just as soon as this train stops I'm going to get off and go find my mother." *And I'll just keep a good distance in the meantime, too.* Making her way to the far end of the car, where there was some more scattered straw, she sat down.

After a while he said, "But suppose — by some chance — you don't find her?"

The question was already churning in Cindy's mind. She couldn't answer it.

He went on thoughtfully, "It's possible that you might consider it convenient to have an older companion — an escort." Not quite a taunt, but almost. It sent Cindy's thoughts off into a new direction. If he wasn't trying to get rid of her, then he must be up to something. Cindy could always tell when grownups were working some scheme, they got too friendly. Why on earth should he want to be of any help to her? Maybe even had some secret notion when he gave her that boost into the train — she hadn't asked him to!

"I only mention it," he went on, "in case you might get an impulse to skip out while I'm catching up on my sleep." In the moonlight that shafted in through the slats of the car, she could see him darkly, stretching himself out on the straw down there. "Better not make any impetuous decisions. Things come clearer in the morning."

Only what he meant was, *don't try to run away!* Cindy thought — he'd see how fast she could move. Just as soon as they got to Denver. Or somewhere — Right now, out there on every side, nothing but vacant prairies, sighing with night wind.

Miserably she hunched down in the straw, burrowing her head in her arms. Thinking of her mother — the one person in the world who had ever loved her, or that she could love — gone now. Gone. And everybody — everything else — Cindy hated!

3

Cindy wakened with a start. Even before she got her eyes open she remembered where she was — the smelly cattle car, the straw beneath her cheek. But they had stopped. It felt warm, like morning. Blinking wide awake, she rolled over and found that she was covered by a black broadcloth coat.

Nearby in the door of the car sat Durango, feet dangling, elbows on his knees. An odd figure in the midst of the drabness of corrals and sidings; his red and white candy-striped shirt seemed to blaze with color under the morning sun. He still wore the black silk garters on his arms that kept his sleeves high and tight while he was playing the piano; his string tie was black silk, too. A couple of switchmen were staring at him in wonder.

And yet when he glanced at them, their grins became

uncertain. There was just enough shadow of a beard on his lean jaws to give him an air of roughness. The slant of the dark flat-crowned hat — or maybe it was the startling, sharp blue of his eyes against the weathered tan of his face. Something about Durango's look made Cindy quiver a little, too.

Carelessly he called to the men. "Whereabouts can I pick up a train connection to Denver?"

That brought her scrambling up in a hurry. She had taken for granted that this *was* Denver. Now as she peered through the slats of the cattle car, she could see that it was an even smaller town than the one they had left. Not much but a few buildings and a maze of corrals.

One of the switchmen scratched his head. "Well, friend, I reckon they give you the wrong accomy-dations. This here's a spur, don't connect up with anything — just turns around and goes back where it come from. So if you want Denver, you better start shankin' it. Only about a hundred miles up yonder." He nodded toward the northwest and a distant profile of mountains, pale blue against a paler sky. The sagebrush wastes were already beginning to look hot under the sun out there.

As the switchmen moseyed off down the track, Durango glanced over his shoulder at Cindy. "I was afraid of that, when we pulled into this place just now. We should have changed cars last night when all that switching went on."

Cindy only vaguely remembered some shunting and shifting, early in the morning hours. "You mean you let us get hitched to the *wrong train!*"

"It was a toss-up in the dark, which was right or wrong." He shrugged. "Don't look so shocked. If you're going to forsake the proper world of Kansas for this less proper life of the hobo you'll have to get used to some little uncertainties." He stood up and put on his coat, brushed the straw from his dark trousers.

Climbing down out of the car they walked across to a watering trough near the cattle pens. There was a pump nearby where they washed. As Cindy splashed the cold water on her face it brought her wide awake — and sorer than ever, to think that she'd slept so hard last night, she'd missed the chance to slip away from this man and get on the right train. By now, she'd probably have been with her mother . . .

As they walked out of the railroad yards, Durango ahead of her, Cindy felt the surge of loneliness threaten to come on again and fought it off. Tried instead to think: *How does anybody get from here to Denver?* Unless you have a horse! She'd just spotted some in an enclosure at the edge of the stock yards. Running over, she swung up onto the bars of the gate. Beautiful mustangs, they snorted and bunched on the far side of the corral, pricking their ears at her.

"They hardly look broken, to me," Durango called, as he walked on. "Besides, for borrowing horses, you're likely to get hanged."

For a minute Cindy swung there on the gate. She really didn't want to go with him. But the switchmen were watching her, and she hurried on. Durango was heading toward the little row of buildings that made up the town. As she caught up she said, "I wasn't going to steal one. Don't you have any money?"

"About enough to buy us breakfast. If you're hungry."

She was starving, but she didn't want to admit it to him. "No thank you."

"Well, I am. And you'd best stick close to me — people in these little towns are suspicious of strangers."

It was true, all right. The old cattlemen who sat around the dining room of the hotel drinking coffee, talking in their dry old voices, suddenly lapsed into silence when Cindy and Durango walked in. It made her uneasy, to have them stare like that.

But worse yet, while they were waiting to be served she caught Durango eying her. And he glanced away so fast, she *knew* he was figuring something. Just the way his fingers drummed on the table. All at once, from being undecided, he seemed to have some idea. As soon as the waiter brought their breakfast, he tossed off his coffee and stood up.

In a low voice he said, "Pull your hat down further over your eyes and take your time. I've got to go get a shave." And to the waiter he added, "Give my little brother anything else he wants. I'll be back in ten minutes." Walked on out before either Cindy or the man could say a word.

She stared at his neglected plate — and he had claimed he was hungry! She had an idea, of course, just what had occurred to him. This was his chance to get away from her. Slowly she began to eat her own breakfast, thinking it was just as well. She could get along without him *fine*. She'd — she'd just — And yet those horses did look pretty wild. And a hundred miles was a long way to walk. She couldn't quite picture it, not without a couple of canteens of water, at least. If she could just find somebody with a wagon, going to Denver — someone who wouldn't be suspicious of a boy asking for a ride —

Right now, though, she was pretty sure, from the way the waiter was staring a hole in her, that he'd guessed she wasn't really anybody's brother. She had just finished her last bit of ham and was thinking how to act — get up and stroll out the door carelessly — when he came and laid a piece of paper down on the table. The check! She'd forgot, they wouldn't let her out of here until it was paid.

So Durango had played her an even dirtier trick than she'd figured. He knew they probably would make her wash dishes or something, to earn her breakfast — long enough for him to get away. She didn't care much, except that she'd have liked to kick his shins for him. The only thing was, when these people found out that she'd been deserted, Cindy had an idea they would start figuring out something to do with her. Grown people never just leave you alone and let you decide what to do, yourself.

Casting about for some way to gain time, she called the waiter. "I'd like some hot cakes, please." Her voice sounded brittle and thin in the quiet room. He cocked an eyebrow, but he went away to get them.

While she ate the flapjacks slowly, she knew she should try to work out a plan, but she kept thinking bitterly about Durango. No question now — he was gone for good. It had been over half an hour since he'd left. She wasn't even surprised that he'd do such a thing. It was just like all the rest that she'd seen of men in the past. They scorn a woman. They either walk off and leave you, or they plot how to make money off of you.

There'd been plenty of times it had been proven, these past few hard years. Like the foreman of the mill where her mother had worked — he'd set his clock to run slow, so that the girls had to work extra long every day. Cindy was even glad when the depression ruined his business. Except that right then Grandma had died and the old house had to be sold. They'd had to sell it awfully cheap, too — they were almost out of money.

It had seemed so lucky when the nice hotel manager had given them a back room to live in and let them eat in the hotel kitchen while her mother worked there as a chambermaid. Except that at the end of the month he

26

gave them a bill for the room and meals that was more than her mother's whole wages came to.

That was when Jill Ferris had decided to go west, to Kansas, and try for work. The cattle towns were booming since the railroads were built. There was no depression there, but it still was hard for a woman to make much of a wage. Even this last job — the dance hall manager would pay only seven cents a dance. That's why they never could save anything.

Anxiously Cindy wondered how much money her mother had. It couldn't be much — and she didn't have a cent herself. With a sinking fear she tried to think how on earth they were ever going to find each other again, in all this endless country. Out the window of the dining room she could see the stretches of gray sand and sage, swelling like a huge sea about to swallow this little town.

And then her lagging spirits quickened. Along the rutted street, Durango was coming back, hurrying. He strode in, tossed two silver dollars on the table for the waiter and beckoned Cindy to come on. Even as she followed him, relieved to be out of there, she began to size up this new turn of events.

"Where are we going?" she asked breathlessly, as she hurried to keep up.

"There's no stage from here to Denver," he said, "but I've got us a couple of tickets on the one to Pueblo. They're holding it for us. Next trip out is day after to-morrow, so we're lucky to have caught this one." And

Cindy saw the coach waiting in front of the Wells Fargo office, its six horses stamping, ready to run.

No time to ask any more questions. They climbed inside, the door was pulled shut, and the horses plunged off at a gallop. The road was so rough that for a while Cindy could only hang onto the strap and try not to get thrown into the laps of the passengers sitting in the opposite seat. But as she got used to the bumps and jolts, she began to wonder again.

Why was Durango doing all this for her? And where did he get the money? Must have more than he pretended, just to leave all that change for the waiter. Besides, he'd been up to something while he was gone. All that time — and he didn't even get a shave. It came over Cindy that maybe it was part of a different scheme, leaving her that way in the dining room. Not so he could escape from her, but so that she couldn't escape from *him!*

And taking her to some place called Pueblo — wherever that was. She looked out the window anxiously and her doubts sharpened. It seemed to her they were going in the wrong direction. The switchman had pointed north — she had to look back over her shoulder to see the high peaks up that way. Suddenly she was sure, the stage was heading south. Away from Denver!

She stole a look at Durango, sitting beside her, with his hat pulled down over his eyes. But the hard line of his jaw was set, he was wide awake. Straight lips tight-pressed in a sort of satisfaction. He knew what he was doing. Far from trying to get rid of her, he was taking her with him somewhere, for some reason. No matter how he might pretend he wasn't even thinking about her, Cindy knew she was in worse trouble than she'd even dreamed.

4

Pᴜᴇʙʟᴏ was a hot, teeming, strange town of dirty
shacks and big warehouses, huts built of mud brick, and
tall Spanish-looking buildings that cast long shadows in
the evening sun. Churches, with their thin white
crosses — they were exactly like the pictures of the
Jesuit missions in Cindy's history book. But most of the
town was lowly and filthy and sweltering.

The people were a strange lot too — some well-
dressed, even rich-looking men with fine leather boots,
while others were nearly in rags. Bearded old codgers
with picks slung across their shoulders, teamsters
cracking their long whips — they thronged the streets.
Here and there a handsome Spaniard or two; Cindy had
seen a few of those back in Kansas.

But this was a far cry from the little cattle town and its cowhands with their pranks. There was a hardened toughness about these people, a boldness, as if they had walked up and down the world and seen the worst of it.

With dusk coming on, the pitch of noise began to rise — a sound of simmering revelry, harsh laughter that made Cindy shiver. The few women who strolled along the street were brazen creatures, not the kind you'd ask for a favor. That had been her first notion, to slip away and find some kind lady — someone like her mother — who would help her get to Denver. But she could see it wasn't going to be that sort of place.

In spite of her distrust of Durango, she kept close to him, at least until she could get her bearings in all this strangeness. He seemed at home here, walked along briskly, down one street and along another until they came to a small hotel.

As they went in, he asked abruptly, "Are you hungry?"

Cindy shook her head. They'd had supper about three o'clock when the stage had stopped to change horses; the food was still lumped up in her stomach. She kept trying to figure out what he was up to. Warily she hung back, watching as he talked with the desk clerk, then signed the register . . . counted out some money. He'd taken a room! Cindy braced herself to run. Because if there was one thing she was *not* going to do, it was to go into any room alone with him.

As Durango turned and came over to her, she got set to dash for the door. He seemed to sense it and stopped short, out of arm's reach of her. His blue eyes flared brighter as if some fire had been turned up behind them.

"Hold on!" he warned, soft and sharp. They were alone in the lobby; the clerk had gone back into his office. Durango went on speaking, so quietly his voice hardly scratched the stillness. "Oh, you can run, of course. But think — where would you go? The world is hard enough on foundlings at best. If you fell into mercenary hands — a gambler or bullwhacker, or worse, a Taos trader — you'd find life could be crueler than you've ever imagined." The thin thread of words seemed to tighten around Cindy like a snare.

"At least consider the dangers — at your leisure." And he flipped her the key. Cindy caught it, hardly realizing what she did. With a slight twist of a smile he added, "Room 207 — all yours until tomorrow morning. I won't bother you; I've got to see about a job, make some money to pay our way to Denver. I know the owner of a variety house here, which should be good for a few nights' work. Meanwhile you might as well get some sleep. Lock yourself in and don't open the door to anyone." He turned away, then added over his shoulder, "I'll be here in the lobby around breakfast time, if you decide to join me."

When he was gone Cindy still stood gripping the key. He'd sounded — even — friendly. As if it had been a lot of silly imagination for her to think that he was plotting something. If he was, how could he dare trust her? Just leave her like this with the only key to the room . . . ? Maybe he really was going to look for a job.

And yet she had to remember that if he had wanted to go to Denver, himself, he could have just stayed with the others and ridden there in comfort. So this was probably more of his trickery. Sometimes when men were lying their worst, they were smiling their nicest — she'd heard her mother say that, often enough.

Even if she did lock herself in, Cindy was thinking that she'd have to come out some time, and he'd be there waiting. And then — then — At least, she thought, she should follow him a little way and see what he might be up to.

She started for the front door of the hotel, but the desk clerk was suddenly ahead of her. He'd come back out of his office quickly to block her way, looking down his nose as grown-ups do.

"Come now, let's be a good lad and mind our older brother. Up to bed with you, bucko!" He pointed to the stairs, then suddenly cocked his head, eying her more closely. "You're a pretty one, aren't you? No wonder it was worth an extra five-dollar gold piece to the gent, to make sure his little *sister* doesn't wander off and come to harm. Now then, upstairs with you, Miss!"

Cindy turned as if to obey, and he started back around the desk — too confidently. She whirled and ran for the door before he was aware of it — out into the street — dodged between two plodding freight wagons, causing the teams to shy and the drivers to curse. Down a side street, up over a wall and into a courtyard, across it and out by way of an iron gate into an alley — she paused there, panting, to listen for the sound of a chase. But if there was any, it was lost far behind. This narrow passage between the old buildings was quiet and remote.

Holding her side, where she'd almost got a stitch, she tried to get her wind and think whether she'd done right or not. But for all that this town frightened her, it scared her a lot worse to think that Durango could lie like that. Looking her right in the eye, he'd made out that he didn't have any money, and yet he'd just given the hotel man a gold piece to keep watch on her.

Five dollars! With that and all the rest he'd spent on the room and the coach tickets and their breakfast that morning, he could surely have bought them a horse, back there at the end of the railroad line. Even if they'd had to ride double, they could have been nearly to Denver by now. So if he didn't want to take her there, he must have something else in mind, just as she had suspected. Bringing her to this dangerous town, with bullwhackers and gamblers — she didn't even know what a Taos trader looked like!

As panic threatened to swamp her, Cindy fought it

off and tried to think, *What would Mother do?* Whenever Jill Ferris got in a tight spot it just made her hold herself a little taller, more ladylike. She would walk right in somewhere and ask for a job and get it. And do her work better than anyone else. Cindy tried to stiffen up inside, to carry herself more confidently as she ventured out of the alley and along the unfamiliar streets.

It was almost full dark by now, which helped — less likely that people would notice she was a girl and pretty young. In this heartless, man's world, she couldn't even think what sort of job she should look for.

About the only work she'd ever done was around the stables back in Kansas. The boys had let her fill the feedbags and even walk the horses sometimes, when they came in hot. But they'd hardly have given her a job for pay. In fact they had snickered when she'd just asked them to let her ride the beautiful stallion they had. "He's too much horse, even for an ornery little filly like you," they'd said. *Men!* She detested the lot of them.

Angrily she trudged on along the crooked streets, glancing in at the doors of dim-lit cellars from which came the wail of songs sung in a strange tongue. And even less inviting places — in one narrow hole-in-the-wall she heard the clink of silver and a voice chanting, "Who'll go me twenty? Twenty, gents — ace of hearts — who'll go me twenty?" Cindy rushed past and turned down the next side street.

35

It was dark except for the light of a lantern swinging over a door halfway along the block. She was almost to it when she saw someone sitting on the step in the shadows — a boy about her own age. Keeping an eye on him, she started to walk on past, then hesitated.

A sign on the wall caught her eye: HIRING. And in smaller letters beneath: SUPES WANTED. She looked up at the building curiously — a large windowless brick hall. This seemed to be the side entrance.

"What's a supe?" she wondered, more to herself than to the boy.

"I'm one," he said, "and just you mind your own business, bub."

That kind of remark always put Cindy's back up. And there was something odd about him. Even though he was trying to keep out of the light, she could see that his cheeks were ghastly pale. And his lips, dark red.

"Just quit your staring," he ordered loudly. "Go on, get! You don't belong on this street — I never seen you before." But as he stood up menacingly, the light fell on his face and Cindy saw that it was white as if it had been dusted with flour. Or powder! That was it! His lips had rouge on them too — he looked as artificial as a doll.

"You're a pretty one!" Cindy giggled — she just couldn't help it.

"Don't you laugh at me!" All at once he lunged at her. She ducked — sheer instinct, though she hadn't really fought any boys since she was little. He jabbed again and landed a sharp one. Suddenly her whole anger against the tribe of bullying menfolk surged up and Cindy let go with a wild free-swinging blow that caught him on the nose. The boy staggered back with a yell that seemed to bring people flying from the building. They rushed out so swiftly that Cindy was surrounded.

"What the deuce!" Several of them clustered about the boy. "Little William's hurt!"

As Cindy made a move to slip away, a hand caught her by the collar and she looked up into a face so weird, she nearly strangled. Towering above her was a tall, gaunt man, his boney features powdered that unearthly white, and his eyes terrible, outlined in greenish paint. The others too, half a dozen men and women — their faces were like masks, rouged and accented with dark lines around the eyes. They were dressed in odd, elegant clothing. Even the little ejaculations they made sounded eerie.

"Unmerciful Providence!" One of the women was twittering over the boy. "The wretched child has got himself a bloody nose!"

"You were told not to leave the theater," one of the men said sternly.

"I got hot! It's blamed stuffy in there!" the boy yelled. "Anyhow, it's all your fault, makin' a feller put this stuff all over his face. I won't be in your cussin' old play, I'm goin' home." Shoving through the little group, he went stomping off up the street. It threw them into a flurry of agitation.

"Oh dear!"

"What on earth shall we do?"

"How's the time?"

"Two minutes to go 'til Act Four."

"And no 'Little William' . . ."

"Stop this foolishness." It was the man holding Cindy who spoke for the first time. The dreadful deep resonance of his voice was like the shudder of a gong, quieting the others. "Of course we have our 'Little William.'" He shook Cindy slightly. "Listen to me, you young rascal, you've caused us a near disaster. But you can make amends. We've a scene to do which requires the presence of a child. Do your part well, and the pay will be twenty-five cents."

Even as he spoke he was marching her into the gloom of the building. As the others followed, shutting the door behind them, he added ominously, "Lock it, this time."

5

INSIDE THE HALL Cindy could just make out the confusion of scenery that crowded the whole rear of the place. But now the tall man had turned her over to two women who hustled her into a tight little dressing room. There, by the light of a smoking kerosene lantern, they sat her down at a table cluttered with powder dishes and rouge pots, waxey green and blue pencils, and brushes in jars of murky liquid. All around the big mirror hung a collection of wigs. The women themselves wore wigs and rich-looking costumes, and so much artful paint on their faces that Cindy couldn't tell what they were really like.

One of them was delving in a trunk nearby, while

the other dipped up a gob of gooey stuff on her fingers and stripped off Cindy's hat.

"Maud! It's a girl!"

For a minute they both stared at her in dismay.

"Never mind, she'll do. She's got to, or Brutus will have our skins! Get on with it, Lorna."

In the mirror Cindy was watching the gruesome transformation of her face. First a coating of grease and now a heavy layer of powder. She'd heard about plays — her mother had told her of seeing some, long ago. But she'd never imagined that actors got themselves up like this! And yet if it meant the chance to earn twenty-five cents — she kept thinking about these supes they were going to hire.

"Why do I have to look so awful?" she mumbled as the woman brushed great dark-brown shadows under her eyes.

"Because in this scene you're supposed to be dying," Lorna told her. "Let us hope fervently you can do it half well!"

"You have only one line." Maud had brought over a loose white nightgown and was stuffing Cindy's arms into the sleeves. "You say: 'Papa has gone for her now.' Then you die, it's very simple."

"What does it mean, though?" Cindy asked, puzzled.

"Oh, it's really a stupid line." Lorna kept fussing around, putting sickly green touches here and there on her face. "And the story's too complicated to explain. Just try to remember the words."

"Papa has gone for her now?" Cindy repeated.

"Dreadful!" snapped Maud. "We'll have to tell her some of it. Look, child, it's like this: You're Little William and your parents have long been separated. You've been raised by your father to think his second wife is your mother. But she isn't — your real mother is 'Lady Isabel' who has come back to your deathbed disguised as a nurse. Now, when she says the word *mother*, that's your cue. You think she means the woman you thought was your mother, who really isn't your mother, and you say 'Papa has gone for her now.' You see?"

Cindy certainly didn't.

"And don't forget that you're dying. You're weak — limp — " Lorna closed her eyes and swayed back and forth, fluttering her hands. " 'Papa . . . has gone . . . for her . . . now . . .' "

A knock at the door interrupted them, and a man called. "Little William scene, coming up — one minute."

"Right away!" Maud settled a floppy nightcap on Cindy's head. "At least she looks the part somewhat more than that lusty little boy." And each taking her by the arm they hurried her out of the dressing room.

The tall man was waiting for them, holding aside the draperies to let them through onto the back of the stage. It was in semi-darkness, shut off from the audience by the heavy curtain in front. From beyond it, came the sound of voices — a massive buzzing noise as if there were hundreds of people out there, waiting for the next scene to begin.

Meanwhile here in the gloom of the stage there was a terrific scurrying, people carrying off pieces of drawing-room furniture while others brought on the trappings of a bedroom. All done so silently, it was amazing. They had placed a couch in the center. Before she knew it, Cindy found herself bundled onto it and covered with a blanket.

"Lie still and wait . . ."

The actors had gathered over to one side around a woman she hadn't seen before, a dark, willowy figure in a flowing black gown and long veil. Cindy guessed that this must be "Lady Isabel." Her questions cut through the murmur of the others.

"What? A girl?"

"Never mind . . . going to look the part perfectly."

"This is most exasperating! Have you shown her exactly how to die?"

". . . not much time . . ."

". . . may need to be prompted . . ."

"What in the name of heaven are you trying to do — ruin me?" the woman demanded in a furious whisper.

"Enough!" The tall man's voice was only a deep, quiet vibration, but the bickering stopped. "A good actress cannot be so easily wrecked. I'm sure you'll be able to handle this little difficulty. In your places, now — "

They scattered silently, leaving the woman in black alone. She walked across with an angry silken swishing of skirts to seat herself in a chair close beside the couch. Cindy was sorry she was a girl and going to ruin things, but there was no time for a word with the lady. Because the curtain was going up — slowly, unevenly, in little jerks.

The stage came to life, by the light of a row of candles. They stood all across the front in tin sconces that reflected their flickering flames — a wall of soft brilliance, separating the make-believe world of the play from the dark ranks of the audience. Though Cindy was aware of the people out beyond, the bedroom scene around her was a pool of warmth. It suddenly seemed real, especially when the actress began to speak.

No irritation about her now; her voice thrilled with sorrow as she lamented the sadness of fate. Her life was ruined, and it was all the fault of some man — that was clear enough. Cindy had never dreamed that a play could be so true! She was filled with acute sympathy, even if she didn't understand it all.

Finally, with heart-rending sadness, Lady Isabel worked up to a pitch of anguish: *"If ever retribution came to woman, it has come to me now! I can no longer bear it. I shall lose my senses. Oh, William! in this last dying hour, try to think I am your — mother."*

The least emphasis on that last word and Cindy remembered — it was her turn. As she hesitated, from somewhere close by, the words were whispered to her in the faintest breath of a whisper. She tried to repeat them weakly, as Lorna had told her: "*Papa . . . has gone for her . . . now.*"

Lady Isabel let out another moan: "*No, not that woman! Look at me, William. I am your mother!*"

Abruptly she cast aside her veil — Cindy was struck breathless. The beautiful face bending over her was full of such compassion, she embraced Cindy so lovingly, for an instant everything got mixed up. The play was all confused with the real torment of loneliness. Clinging to the lady fiercely, Cindy burst into tears.

Softly in her ear the actress whispered, "Now, die — quickly!"

Struggling for control, filled with sudden determination not to ruin anything, Cindy did it. In a fling of arms, she fell back limp and lifeless.

With a wail, Lady Isabel clutched her tighter, crying: "*Dead! And never called me 'Mother.'*"

A roar broke out around them. The audience was shouting, stamping, as the curtain came down. Cindy lay stunned on the couch and listened. Slowly it dawned on her that the people out there were applauding. She had done all right.

When it was all over, Cindy could see that the others were downright pleased with her. As they gathered around backstage, Lorna kept pulling and patting at her, and Maud gruffly announced that she was a regular trouper. "Lady Isabel" made a curious reference to ham, but she sounded good-humored, especially when one of the men told her she had shown superb poise. Then the tall actor walked over to join them and they grew quiet.

"So the lad turns out to be a lass," he remarked, looking down at Cindy. She could just see the gleaming eyes far back under his jutting brows. "Your services were satisfactory, Miss." And he offered her a quarter with a graceful gesture of two long fingers. "Ladies and gentlemen, let us disperse. We have the farce to do, you know."

Cindy took the coin. Never had a piece of money felt so good in her palm. "Sir — " she spoke out on impulse, in spite of her apprehension of the man. The others turned, surprised, and waited to hear what she might say.

"Sir," she repeated, "could I come back tomorrow night and die again for another quarter?"

"We'll not be playing *East Lynne* in this town again. In fact the troupe will only be here one more day. However," Brutus regarded her thoughtfully, "if you return tomorrow, perhaps we can find use for your services in some capacity. If you will show up for rehearsal in the afternoon, I shall double your wage."

Fifty cents was a terrible, attractive sum. Urgently Cindy said, "Couldn't I do some more for you tonight? I'd be glad to help you carry the furniture around or anything — "

"Are you in some sort of financial straits, my dear?" Lorna asked her kindly.

"Worse than that, I don't have any money. Except this quarter," Cindy added in a rush, "and my mother's gone — they took her off to Denver. I got separated from her when they ran us out of Kansas and he brought me down here — Durango did — and I don't know why. But he's a cool, tricky kind of man, he's a piano player and he's been figuring something — "

"Just a moment, young lady." The actor interrupted with sudden interest. "Begin at the beginning of this tragic tale."

As they drew around, listening, Cindy was so relieved by their sympathy that the whole story came tumbling out, right on down to the way Durango had tried to trap her, renting that room this evening, to get her to wait for him. "Only I ran away instead, so I don't have any place to go, and I was wondering if I could maybe sleep on that couch when you're done with it tonight," she finished hopefully.

They all seemed marvelously concerned. "Lady Isabel" turned to the tall man with obvious emotion. "Brutus, a piano player — "

"Exactly," he cut in on her swiftly. "The fellow must be dealt with. Where did you say he pretended to be going, child?"

"To look for work in a variety theater. But he's an awful liar," Cindy warned.

"Ah, poor dear, you've been quite sadly treated."

Lorna put a comforting arm about her shoulders. "It's this wild country we're in — a far cry from New York, where people are genteel."

But now one of the younger men looked at his pocket watch. "Six and a half minutes . . ."

"Yes, and I can hear the audience growing restive." Brutus nodded. "For the moment, Lorna, you may take charge of the child. Ralph, you'll do my role in the farce tonight. I'm off to see about this mischievous musician!"

And from the grim manner in which he strode away, Cindy — almost — felt sorry for Durango.

6

Iт was like a dream — a wonderful, wishful daydream where you imagine you're rich and can just order people like hotel managers to send breakfast up to your room . . .

"Set the tray over there, please," Lorna told the waiter.

Sleepily Cindy rolled over in bed. It was a real brass bedstead with big knobs and curlicues and the featheriest mattress she'd ever slept on. Everything was so luxurious. Lorna in a ruffley dressing gown was pouring the coffee into pretty little cups.

She was a sprightly woman with soft, shining, silvery hair. Cindy thought she hardly seemed old enough to be that gray, for her face was slender and charming, even with all its tiny smile-wrinkles, and her manner was almost girlish. Her hands hovered over the coffee cups, graceful as two white flowers.

"It looks woefully strong," she said. "Shall I put in extra cream?"

"You know I take mine black," Maud answered shortly, without glancing up from the newspaper she was reading. A heavy-set woman with bold features, she seemed even more formidable in the bright morning light than she had the evening before. Without the paint on her face she looked quite old; her bun of wirey hair was almost white. But it had been black once; her thick brows were still dark and there was a brown fuzz upon her upper lip that added to the naturally somber look of her face.

From the comfortable depths of the bed Cindy studied her critically. She didn't quite like Maud — the way she had bossed everybody around last night after they got back here. Making Cindy take a bath, scrub down to the quick, and even wash her hair before she could go to bed.

Now, though, her grumpy look warmed up a little as she began to read aloud from the paper. "Listen to this: 'The Thespian Theater was literally jammed last night with the best element of Pueblo's intelligentsia who were rewarded by an excellently performed tragedy entitled *East Lynne.*'"

"How good of them." Lorna hurried over to read it with her. "Did they mention any of us?"

"Brutus, of course. And Helene — 'The part of the

doomed wife, Lady Isabel, was played to perfection by Mademoiselle Helene Paree, whose powerful rendition gave the role great dramatic depth.' "

As Maud was reading, the door of the next room swung open, and the beautiful young woman stood there listening. So her real name was Helene. Cindy savored it, marveling at how lovely she was without all the rouge and powder. She had been fixing her long, honey-blond hair and still held the brush in her hand as she listened to Maud with her head a-tilt.

" 'Great dramatic depth,' " she repeated. Then suddenly smiled with a slight tolerance. "That's fairly well put for a little junk-town paper. I hope Brutus will be inspired to give me a few more roles that I can get my teeth into." She tossed the hairbrush aside and drew on a pink silk wrapper over her nightgown, then walked across to the table to read over Maud's shoulder. "Of course, it has its disadvantages to be so well received. I hope it won't mean we'll extend our stay in this ugly little burg."

Maud gave a sort of snort. "One good house is hardly a season. We've probably exhausted Pueblo's entire 'intelligentsia' with a few mule skinners thrown in."

"They should have been thrown out," Helene remarked, pouring herself some coffee. "All that dreadful noise from the gallery."

"From what I've read of the rest of the towns in this Territory, we're in for a good deal worse." Maud looked troubled as she turned the pages of the paper.

"Shootings, stage hold-ups, wild Indians, I don't know what-all!"

"And crude accommodations in tumbledown flea-bags," Helene glanced around the little room scornfully.

"This is a good clean place," Maud retorted, as if she'd somehow taken the remark personally. "It's not easy to choose the right hotel, what with some people complaining all the time and the rates so high, here in the West. If there's one thing Brutus hates, it's hotel bills eating into his profits."

"And *I* hate Brutus," Helene said airily. "If he doesn't provide us with first-class living arrangements, he will find himself minus his *première actérienne!*" There was a tartness about the last words that brought a twitch of anger to Maud's face. Abruptly she got up and went out into the next room, shutting the door behind her with a sharp snap.

"She's really in a mood, isn't she?" Helene began to scan the paper. "Probably irritated that she didn't get a mention here. Maybe she should have played the part of the villain. She's certainly got the moustache for it."

Lorna clicked her tongue in reproof, but Cindy was smiling into the pillows. She couldn't help admiring anyone as young as Helene who could stand up to older people and not get squelched. And you could tell she wasn't the least bit afraid of that Brutus or anyone else.

By contrast, Lorna seemed almost timid. "You know

why Maud's upset — she always gets worried when Ollie's gone. And he should have been back from Denver two days ago."

That brought Cindy upright in bed. "Who's in Denver?"

"Well, here's our little supe!" Helene smiled across at her indulgently. "Already getting the hang of theater life, sleeping late like a prima donna."

And Lorna came over to the bed to kiss her lightly. "How do you feel, dear? My, you must have been tired. I doubt you moved once all night."

"Then I'll sleep with her next time," Helene remarked. "Maud kicks as if the bloodhounds were snapping at her heels. How Ollie stands it — "

"Who's Ollie and why did he go to Denver?" Cindy insisted, all clinched up inside at just the mention of the place.

"He's Maud's husband, our advance agent," Lorna explained. "He goes ahead of us to arrange for theaters and post the bills, rent rooms and all that."

"You mean you're all going to Denver?" It was such a piece of news, Cindy could hardly believe her luck. "That man — would he give me some sort of job so I could go with you?" Cindy looked at them imploringly. "Can I go talk to him right now?"

"If you'll hurry and dress. We'd all better put on our running slippers." Lorna glanced at the little gold watch on the bureau. "Rehearsal in less than an hour."

"And if Brutus refers just once more to the Green

Room Rules" — Helene picked up the newspaper and folded it — "I shall stuff this column right down his chops."

They found Cindy a dress to wear; they had whole trunks full of costumes. And though it made her uneasy — you just can't run as fast in patent-leather shoes and a dress — all the same, it was rather pretty. Blue, with a smart little black velvet collar, and Lorna tied her hair back with a velvet ribbon. Cindy had never cared for it that way, hanging down her back like a dark, wild horsetail, but Helene gave it a twist with her curling iron and proclaimed that Cindy looked most flirtatious.

That steadied her a little; it made her feel older. And she thought she was going to need that, when it came to dealing with this Brutus.

As she stood with Lorna outside his office she had to concentrate hard on her mother and on her troubles, to brace up enough to face him. And when he opened the door, Cindy almost swallowed her tongue.

He was just as tall as he'd seemed last night, with a great shock of tawny hair — it sprang from his high forehead and flowed backward in a mass. Even without the theatrical paint, his face was austere and compelling, hollow cheeks beneath the fierce bone structure that framed his eyes. They were reddish too — almost the same burnt color as his hair.

"Come in, young lady," he said, and Cindy quivered

as if the deep tones of the powerful voice had plucked at her. She was aware that Lorna had left them, that she was alone with him in this narrow room, but she couldn't tear her look away as he studied her soberly.

"So you would like to join our troupe," he mused, "at least until such time as you find your unfortunate parent, wherever she may be."

"She's in Denver," Cindy managed to blurt out pretty strongly. "And Lorna says you're going there, and I'd work hard — I wouldn't eat much." She broke off, for Brutus had shaken his head.

"The matter of your sustenance," he said slowly, "is less important than the question of — your maturity."

Cindy's heart sank. He meant that she was too young.

"The theater is no place for childishness of any kind," he went on, bracing his fingertips together as he considered her. "It is an enterprise in which we each have our responsibilities. Any failure of one can bring ruination on us all, as you saw last night. You may imagine what chaos the absence of Little William would have created, had you not been handy to the occasion. The boy had disobeyed explicit orders to stay close to the stage. Of course, he was merely a local lad with no sense of obligation to the rest of us . . ." He paused and eyed her.

"I wouldn't run off when you needed me," Cindy promised.

"I might add that the troupe must work in complete

cooperation, in spite of personal differences. Petty quarrels, animosities must be forgotten when we gather here at the theater."

"But I like everybody," Cindy protested, and privately vowed she would *try* to like them if they'd help her get to Denver.

"We — and all other dramatic troupes — pursue our difficult profession under a strict set of rules," Brutus went on, the words rumbling out like a roll of thunder. "They are called The Green Room Rules. In practice, the backstage is the 'green room' and when we enter it, we are all subject to the articles. If you are to join us you must agree to abide by them without question."

Cindy nodded urgently. She had no idea what they might be, but she'd never been afraid of rules. They only meant you got scolded if you did something wrong. And Brutus was sounding as if he were maybe going to hire her in spite of her youngness. Right then she'd have agreed to anything.

"In that case you may consider yourself employed." Brutus sat down at his desk, shoved aside the paint jars and wax pencils to open a ledger. "We shall enter you as a supernumerary, of unspecified duties, with weekly wages of five dollars and keep."

The sum shocked Cindy speechless. She'd never had five dollars of her own in her life. The most she had hoped for was three-fifty, which was fifty cents a day and had seemed a fortune to her last night. It was so extra generous of him — abruptly she became suspicious. There must be something wrong here; nobody had ever done her such a favor before. As she listened to the scratch-scratch of his quill pen in the book, it came over her!

Brutus glanced up in time to glimpse the doubt in her eyes. "Well, Lucinda, what is it?"

"How did you know my name, to write it in your book?" she asked.

"Ah, yes. That was divulged in my conversation last evening with your curious acquaintance, Durango, the musician."

The prick of fear dug deeper inside her. "What did you — ? You didn't tell him I was here!"

"For the most part we talked of other things, of music and the theater. Which reminds me . . ." He got up and went to the door of the office to speak to someone outside. "You may begin the rehearsal. I'll be with you in a moment." Turning back to Cindy he added, "You shall see what a rare adjunct it is to the success of any production — a suitable melodic background. Ever since our violinist and his accompanist quit — in St. Louis a few weeks ago, to pursue a career on a riverboat — we have been quite desolate."

But Cindy was hardly listening. For as Brutus spoke, through the half-open door came a tentative music. Tinkling chords, struck with a moody grace — they were like slow-spoken words. And she knew! Somehow she knew — Drawn by the sound, she ventured out to where she could see. Durango sat at the piano just below the stage, carelessly fingering the keys, a dark expressionless figure amid the members of the troupe who had crowded around him in excitement.

"A strange fellow," Brutus remarked. He had followed her and stood watching too. "But not likely to do you any harm, especially with all of us around to protect your tender young person. And the fact is, he plays a devilish good piano!"

Cindy bit her lip. It was all she could do to hold back a furious answer. Because it was plain enough, Durango had tricked her again! And whether or not they knew it, they had all helped.

7

"WILL YOU LISTEN, please?" The young man was getting impatient. But Cindy wasn't worried about him — just a boy, really, not more than sixteen or so. Even if he was Brutus' son, Eric was hardly an image of his father. Lanky, loose-limbed, with awkward light hair that kept falling in his eyes, he seemed to stumble all over himself to do whatever the others told him. When they had assigned him to instruct Cindy in how to make herself useful, he had accepted the job with a sigh.

"In the theater, you've got to stay alert every minute," he was saying. "You've got to listen — "

And she was, but not to him. Cindy was concentrating on the others as they rehearsed against the background of melancholy music from the piano. Trying to rally her thoughts, which were all askew.

Brutus was the one she was trying hardest to figure. Anybody who could act the way he could! In this play, he took the role of a nice old coal miner whose beautiful young wife had deserted him. He seemed so sad and gentle, his voice tremulous as he said: *"Ah, Nelly, I were foolish to think that thou cared for me, rough as I knew myself to be; but I had hoped that thou wouldst have cheered my lonely path through life, and when I were dead, would have dropped a tear over my grave. But it were not to be . . . it were not to be . . ."* It was enough to make your throat get tight. And yet the minute the scene came to an end, he straightened up and was aloof again. Gave a short nod of approval to Durango.

"That was precisely the right strain you struck there, sir. Excellent," he said, with crisp satisfaction.

The pianist tapped two notes with his forefinger, his curious way of saying "Thank you."

And a premonition grew stronger in Cindy — that these two were in complete accord. Brutus was a smart man; both of them were. Too smart for either to fool the other. So it meant that somehow they had come to an understanding, made some bargain that included her. The more she thought about it, the more a nameless fear gripped her.

"You're not paying attention," Eric said sharply,

nudging her. "Please, this is quite important even if it does seem like a small thing."

She tried to listen to what he was telling her, something about making it snow.

"The first scene of the second act takes place in winter, in a house in London," he was saying, as if repeating something he'd already told her. "Our set has two windows — remember — two. You've got to make the snow fall past both of them at once. You'll be up on a stepladder between them with a basket of snow — "

"Real snow?" Cindy asked absently.

"Certainly not! Cotton stuffing — wait, I'll show you." He walked over and searched through the clutter of junk behind the scenery, coming back with a box full of bits of cotton. Rather dirty cotton, it looked as if it had been used to make a lot of winter in its time. "It's up to you to make it look as near as possible like real snow coming down." Eric showed her, dribbling it through his fingers a little at a time.

"Do you usually do this yourself?" she wondered.

"I have," he said. "Somebody has to. Tonight, since you'll be handling it, I'll be able to stay with the stage. That's my main job, prompting. You know, the way I whispered to you when you couldn't remember your line last night?" But he wasn't being mean, in reminding her. Eric was just trying earnestly to do what he'd been told to do — explain things. Another time Cindy might have been grateful. But right now she just wished she could get away for a minute, to think. It

61

was a relief when he handed her the box of cotton.

"You may want to practice a little. We'll try it from the ladder after a while. Right now I've got to get the supes ready for the next scene."

Cindy watched him hurry off to round up the handful of men who stood gawking on the other side of the stage. Local fellows, they looked fairly fuddled by the strangeness of it all. Supernumeraries — people who aren't really actors, hired on for a night or two to do some little bit of a part or to make up a crowd on stage, when the play called for one. That was a supe, Cindy had found out from Eric. He was explaining the scene to them now, going on in that harassed tone.

"In the play you're a bunch of coal miners — are you all listening? You walk on stage together, you're going with the hero, off to work. And as you march away, you sing this song. It doesn't matter if your voices aren't too good, that'll just make it seem more realistic. Have you learned the words? *'Down in the depths of the darksome mines, we work, we work . . .'* All right then, let's go and practice it with the piano."

Kicking at the skirts that seemed to fuss around her ankles, Cindy walked over to the women's dressing room. It was empty. She went in and closed the door behind her to shut out the buzz of the rehearsal. Sitting down gloomily she considered the box of cotton snow. A silly chore that anyone could do — nothing important, like dying. Even if she had promised Brutus that she'd never slip away when she was needed, she had hardly meant it to include a thing like making it snow. Besides, he'd deceived her — getting her to promise before he told her that he had hired Durango.

Any way she looked at it, there was no choice except to go her own way alone again, no matter how hard it was to leave these nice women. It had been such a warm, comfortable feeling this morning, to lie in bed, listening to their little jokes. Now it made it all the worse to think of dodging and hiding, keeping to the shadows . . . go back to the hotel and slip into boys' clothing again . . .

Cindy stared at herself in the dressing table mirror with a slight misgiving. Because the fact was, it was no wonder the hotel clerk had recognized her for a girl. She'd never been one to primp and pose in front of a looking glass, like some people. Even though her mother had tried to convince her that she was growing pretty and ought to take heed of her looks, Cindy just hadn't felt like it. But now, with this dress on and her hair curled a bit, she realized suddenly how her face and throat were beginning to fill out. It must have been coming on these past few months; the stringy boyish look was disappearing, her whole body getting softer. And right now, when she needed most to be skinny!

She was still sitting there, worrying over it, when the door behind her swung open and Lorna came in, gaily danced across and gave her a hug. "What a blessing! What a pleasure!" She spun around in a little whirl of skirts and dropped Cindy a curtsey. "You're a real good-luck charm, little one! To bring us a pianist who can play so beautifully — gallops and interludes and wonderful slow sad music. Just wait until you do Little William next time, with that piano breaking everybody's heart."

Helene had followed Lorna in. Prettily she said, "When Little Cinders is through being the heroine of the piece, she can give me that place at the mirror."

Cindy started up out of the seat at once. "Well, I *know* Durango's fierce at the piano, but don't you think he's —he's — what do you think of him?" She turned to Helene.

But she was more concerned over a fine hair out of place in her eyebrow. Leaning close to the glass she plucked it out with a pair of little silver tweezers. "Oh yes," she said, when she was satisfied with it, "yes, I must say he's quite good. And we do need the accompaniment. It's simply impossible to create a proper mood without it."

"I'm sure you needn't be afraid of the man," Lorna insisted innocently. "Why, he seems very well-mannered. And so quick to catch the essence of a scene."

Grimly Cindy thought it was probably true; Durango could almost read peoples' minds. He'd know how to please these actors if he wanted to.

"Well, I know he's trying to keep me from my mother," she told them. "*I know it!* And I ought to be up there in Denver right now. She must be dreadful worried about me. Listen, if you could just lend me some money, enough for a coach ticket, I'd send it back to you right away. I promise!" She looked again at Helene, but it was Lorna who answered.

"Why, darling, of course we would, if it were only a matter of the fare. But suppose by some chance your mother wasn't there? She might have already gone back to Kansas to look for you."

Cindy was appalled. Such an idea had never entered her mind.

"They say Denver is a monstrous place," Helene added fastidiously. "The minute you'd set foot off the coach you'd be a prey to all sorts of scandalous fiends. No, Little Cinders, you'd better stay with us. Be a dear and find me my fan — in the trunk, there. Gracious, it's getting beastly warm this afternoon."

"And we must get back to the stage." Lorna glanced at her watch anxiously. "Brutus told us to take only a short intermission. But don't worry, little dear. You're safe as long as you're with us. Oh — ! they're calling the next scene, Helene!"

Lingering at the door of the dressing room Cindy watched them hurrying toward the stage. Everybody was crowded together there to listen to Brutus, who was lecturing them about their elocution. A good time to slip away. Slowly she headed for the side exit, the same door through which she'd been hustled in last night. Opening it quietly, she stepped out into the street.

High afternoon, with the sun sheeting down so blinding hot, Cindy stood a minute blinking. As she paused in the narrow band of shade along the side of the building, she was suddenly aware of someone else standing there a few feet away. Durango — a thread of smoke was rising from the thin black cheroot which he held carelessly.

"Don't look so startled," he said. "I'm not here to block your path of flight. I just stepped out for a smoke."

Cindy couldn't move. But her thoughts were racing — if he saw her leave, he'd go right back in and tell the others.

"You flattered me somewhat, I think, when you described me to Brutus," he went on with that faint mockery. "He thought he was searching for a true desperado. I had to assure him that I'm really a figment of your imagination, a creature of great skulduggeries as yet unconceived. My only sin — the misguided notion to assist you in your troubles."

"You never really wanted to go to Denver!" Cindy burst out passionately. "You can't fool me!"

"You're quite right, I didn't. I don't now. I have no slightest concern for the locality where I happen to find myself at any given moment. All towns look alike after a while. And as for the job of being your keeper, I take great pleasure in giving that up, Miss Ferris, ma'am. Nothing on earth could persuade me to force myself upon you. So if you were planning another mad escape, you may want to save yourself the inconvenience. However, if you do prefer to run — and run and run — you'll get no argument from me. I told Brutus it would be a mistake, to put much trust in your ability to stay in one place. But that's his business. I intend henceforth to mind only my own." Abruptly Durango spun the stub of his cheroot out into the dusty street. Without another look at her he strolled into the building.

With all her breath bottled up tight, Cindy stood and waited. Now it would come, as it had with the hotel manager. He would set someone to follow her, even to bring her back by force. She was determined to be ready with a smooth remark — "I just stepped out for a breath of fresh air" — and yet, as the minutes dragged by and no one appeared, she began to wonder. Could he have meant it this time?

The longer she stood there, the more lonesome the deserted side street seemed. All around was the impersonal hubbub of the town and beyond that, the steep distant mountains looming. On the other hand, right here within this building were people who had befriended her, Lorna, Helene. Maybe they weren't very concerned about helping her find her mother, but Cindy thought she could do that herself if she could just earn this money. In a week or a little more she could walk off and buy herself a ticket, if they hadn't come to Denver by then.

With a rush of surrender she pushed open the door

and ran inside. So he had tried to make them distrust her! She even smiled as she thought that Mr. Durango was in for a surprise.

8

Going north! Today — at last. Cindy skipped along the board sidewalk a few paces ahead of the three women, who moved slowly in the early sunlight. There had been a good deal of sleepy grumbling as they'd gotten dressed. They certainly weren't used to getting up at any such hour as five o'clock.

"We're not billed in Colorado Springs, wherever that may be" — Helene wrinkled her nose slightly — "until the end of this week. So I don't see why Brutus has to rush us off without our rest. Unless, of course, he wants us to come on as the three witches out of *Macbeth*."

"We need rehearsal time, that's why," Maud told her curtly. "We've got to build a larger repertoire. If we're to play a city like Denver, we can't do *East Lynne* every other day or so."

"And *Lost in London* is still woefully ragged," Lorna added, fluttering her hands in a helpless little way she had. "That performance last night just showed how we need to work on it."

"*'Double, double toil and trouble.'*" Helene made a little hex sign at them both. "I thought I was quite dazzling."

Cindy felt like laughing aloud, because she thought so too. It seemed to her that the play last night had been a great success. The audience had shouted and applauded at the end. In the last scene, the heroine had to die, and Cindy, watching from the wings, had been filled with admiration. So elegantly sad, so graceful, the way Helene had sort of oozed down onto the floor, sobbing, "*Forgive . . . forgive . . .*" Cindy thought if she could ever learn to die like that, she'd be proud.

In fact these were really wonderful actors, all of them. Maud had surprised her most, dressing up in man's clothing and a wig and beard, to play a funny character who was always offering to fight somebody. It was usually Ollie's part, they said, but Maud was so gruff and brisk at it, Cindy would never have guessed she wasn't a man. Even now, as she marched along in a stiff broadcloth traveling dress, with a little tailored jacket, it was as if some of the role still clung to her.

"There's Brutus waiting. Hurry up girls," she said as she strode forward, skirts flapping.

The men were gathered in the deserted street in front of the theater. Eric was already busy taking down the bill that had been tacked to the entrance, advertising last night's program. Brutus was discussing something with

Durango. Only Ralph turned to greet the women as they came up.

A handsome young man with wavey auburn hair, he had played the part of the villain last night, but Cindy thought he never seemed truly wicked in it. He was too busy being charming. She didn't care for him much — he kept fawning over Helene.

"Here's our charming queen of hearts," he said now, making an extravagant bow. "Good morning, ladies all."

Brutus swung around then and viewed them severely. "You're late, mesdames."

"Not late enough, sir," Helene told him airily. "You've cost me my beauty sleep."

"Beauty is as beauty does. I wonder that any of you could sleep after that haphazard rendition last evening." He stood towering over them on the theater step, drawing a small notebook from an inner pocket of his coat.

"We're not in the green room now, Brutus," Helene protested.

"Nor am I taking account of your present impertinence, Miss," he said. "Last night provided an ample enough number of infractions of the rules. You, for instance, violated Article One no less than a half-dozen times. May I quote it, to refresh your memory: 'At time of rehearsal or performance the manager is not to be applied to on any matter of personal complaint.' For each breach, fifty cents, to be deducted from your wages."

71

"Go on, then." Helene waved her hand as if to brush the whole business away. "But I shall continue to complain of any annoyance such as that dreadful bunch of supes. They kept whispering all through my lines, I could hardly make myself heard."

Brutus turned to Eric. "The supes were, indeed, in very poor decorum. Didn't you impress upon them the necessity for quiet?"

"Yes, sir." The boy stood looking down at the poster which he held, his face painfully red. "They — don't pay much attention to a — anyone my age."

"It's your job to make them pay attention. Your failure amounts to 'neglect in office or non-observance of duties — ' " Brutus flipped over a page. "And while we're about it, you made quite some disturbance yourself at one point in Act Two. Your voice carried quite through the dialogue on stage—call it 'interruption of performance,' Article Eight — a forfeit of five dollars."

Cindy listened in amazement. He was actually sentencing these people to fines. It made her squirm, because the reason Eric had to raise his voice last night was to call to her, up on the stepladder, that she was being careless with the snow. So maybe Brutus was even going to take some of her own pay away from her.

But instead he spoke to Lorna almost reproachfully. "And you, my dear. For the first time in my memory, you made the stage wait."

"I know, I'm terribly sorry," she murmured.

But that was Cindy's fault, too. Trying to help

72

Lorna with a quick change of costumes, she'd got fumble-fingered and the buttons got buttoned up wrong and had to be done over again. She started to blurt it out, but Lorna nudged her to keep still.

"In spite of all this, they did rather *like* us last night, though." Helene tossed off the remark to no one in particular. She had reached a foot-tapping mood by now.

Brutus glanced at her icily. "Whether or not the audience demands a high quality of theater — I demand it. You will all remember this and work on your parts as we travel north. Meantime, let's get to the business of packing the stage effects. I'll bring the wagons around as soon as Durango and I have managed to locate a piano for sale. No telling whether or not such luxuries will be available in all the theaters we'll be playing."

As Cindy followed the others on into the building, a certain disappointment dimmed the brightness of her earlier feelings. First the embarrassing matter of the scolding they had gotten. And now to find they weren't even going north by stagecoach. Going to poke along in wagons.

And ponderous cumbersome ones, at that, she soon found out. Within an hour they were drawn up at the side door. Most of the heavy scenery went into the four-horse freight van, a big old box of a wagon painted black with gold lettering on the side: BRUTUS BRAITHWAITE'S THESPIANS.

The smaller things, all the little trappings and props,

had to be packed in the trunks. These and the prettiest pieces of furniture were arranged in the other, a plain, drab covered wagon where the women were to ride. Back in Kansas, Cindy had seen these lumbering Conestogas often enough, but of all times to have to travel in one — !

And yet, after the hectic confusion of getting loaded, she was glad enough just to be on the way at last, even if the pace was maddeningly slow. A weary sort of relief settled in, paced to the clip-clop of horses' hooves and the creak of axles. In the afternoon sunlight Pueblo fell gradually behind in the distance until it was just an ugly little clutter back there in the empty land.

Nearer and more personal, somehow, were the mountains now. Huge fists of mountains, knobby with knuckles, that seemed to press down on the rippling sage country. The road was veering toward them, little by little, and sometimes when the hot prairie wind shifted for a minute, a sudden coolness would draft down out of the deep canyons.

A monstrous, huge land. Cindy felt dwindled by it as she sat perched on the tail gate of the wagon. Even the big van back there was only a struggling black speck, falling farther behind as the road grew more hilly.

Crawling back inside the wagon, she found it dim and hot; the front curtains were drawn against the dust. She could just make out the three listless figures — Helene lying on the couch with a damp cloth over her eyes, and Maud and Lorna crowded into close-set chairs. Their shirtwaists were unbuttoned at the throat, their bodies moving slackly with the joggling of the wagon. Maud seemed to be in deep concentration and Lorna looked blankly into space, her lips working slightly as if she were repeating lines to herself.

It was beginning to come clear to Cindy that this wasn't really such a wonderful life they were leading. They seemed all gripped by the demands of their work and their manager. If such a good show as yesterday's wasn't enough, she began to think there would never be any pleasing Brutus. It was too bad, she reflected, but this was always how jobs seemed to turn out. You need one and you're glad to get it, and then it goes mean and unpleasant. Somebody begins to bully you.

All the more, it made her wonder how much silent hardship her mother had borne all these years. And the thought of what she must be going through now, all alone somewhere — Cindy wished she could get out and fly on and on ahead. She picked her way forward to the front of the wagon and slipped out between the curtains, swinging her skirts over to sit on the driver's seat beside Eric. She peered ahead so hard that if wishing could have done any good, Denver would have appeared on the horizon.

"How far are we going today?" she asked restlessly.

The boy was just letting the horses poke along, the reins wrapped around one wrist, while he studied a little yellow-bound booklet. Glancing up at her blankly he repeated, "How far? I don't know." And went back to his reading.

"Do you always go so slow?"

Eric looked up again, a lock of fine light hair falling down across his eyes. "Always? It's hard to say. We haven't traveled like this very long, just since Dodge City. When we got that far we found everything so different from the East. In theaters back home they've got scenery and props on hand. Out here, we're lucky to find a hall with some seats in it. We had to make all our own settings and carry them along."

"But what I mean is, couldn't you send the people on ahead by stagecoach?"

Eric seemed to wince. "Don't let Father hear you say that. It's been an awful argument. In fact one of our actors, Peter, quit and went back to New York just because Father wouldn't agree to it. No, it's better for us all to be together constantly. We haven't been a troupe very long; we need to — to get the feel of each other."

Cindy could tell that he was repeating whatever Brutus had spouted; he was even trying to believe it. Cautiously she said, "Your father's sort of cross, isn't he? I'm sorry he bawled you out just for telling me about the snow last night. That wasn't your fault."

Eric gave her an absent smile. "You haven't heard him get started yet. That's not half what he'll say if I don't get this part memorized." And he turned back to the play.

It surprised Cindy. She'd hardly supposed that he was an actor too. "What kind of part is it?"

Once more Eric looked up, trying to be patient. "I have to understudy Ollie, so if he's delayed on one of these advance trips, I can step into his part. Peter used to do it, but now I've got to. And we're billed to do *Box and Cox* in Colorado Springs. If Ollie doesn't get there in time, I — I — Well, it's a farce and there are even some songs I've got to learn, so I'd better get to work on it."

"I thought we were going to do *East Lynne* again." Cindy was a little disappointed. She'd been gearing herself to do a good job on Little William.

"We are," he said, with a slight tinge of exasperation. "The melodrama comes first and then we finish off with the farce, which is supposed to leave the audience in a state of hilarity, and I've never done it b-b-before and I've really got to b-bone up."

She had noticed that when he got upset, Eric stuttered slightly. She tried to keep quiet for a while. But the question kept getting bigger in her mind until she just had to ask it.

"Why? Why are you all doing this? I mean, working so hard and traveling in wagons and learning all these lines and getting blamed for things and — "

Eric cut in a little sharply. "I can't tell you why the others are here, but as for me — it's obvious. B-Brutus is my father. Naturally I'm going to be in his troupe."

Cindy thought she'd certainly never let that put a

stranglehold on her if she were as old as Eric. "How old are you?" she blurted out.

That question did it. He lost the distracted look and stared at her as if she'd accused him of something. She could see a flash of resemblance to his father as he said, "Old enough to know what I'm doing." And then he looked away fast. "Will you please let me get these lines studied?"

As he bent over the play again Cindy felt distantly sorry for him, because he was near enough to being a mangrown that he could have gone his own way, and he knew it. So it must be about as she'd figured. They were all afraid of Brutus, mightily afraid. Except Helene, maybe, and even she had been fined and was lying down right now with a headache.

All of them, trapped in this hectic pursuit. Cindy was just personally thankful that it wouldn't be long now until she would be free of this odd crew and their fierce master.

9

Brutus was getting more irritated by the minute at that first rehearsal in Colorado Springs. When they had finally arrived there, they'd found that the theater was just a meeting hall with a raised platform at one end. By the time the stage was set there was scarcely room for two people to stand amid the furnishings. Brutus couldn't stride about, waving his arms.

It was that kind of a comedy — an impossible story about a couple of men who'd each been engaged to the same girl and didn't know it. They kept arguing over who would get her money, since she was lost in a shipwreck. A lot of nonsense. It was no wonder Eric had been so troubled, trying to memorize it.

Since Ollie hadn't shown up, the boy was taking the

part of "Box" while his father was "Cox." They kept trading these ridiculous lines as fast as they could talk:

"*The fortune's mine.*"

"*Mine!*"

"*I'll go to law.*"

"*So will I.*"

"*Stop — a thought strikes me. Instead of going to law about the property, suppose we divide it.*"

"*Equally?*"

"*Equally. I'll take two-thirds.*"

"*That's fair enough. And I'll take three-fourths.*"

Cindy glanced at the rest of the troupe. Gathered on the benches out in front, to make up an audience, they looked fairly unhappy about the way it was going. Time after time Brutus stopped the scene.

"No, no, sir, you're not creating the character! Forget that you're Eric, playing 'Box.' *Be* the man. And your elocution is faltering. Remember, you must round off your periods in a pleasant and musical manner."

"When the dialogue is cracking off that fast?" Eric protested.

"Do you presume to question me, boy? Even a single word must be rendered eloquent." Brutus fixed his son with a look that would have driven nails. "We'll take the scene over from the point where you come in. And this time try to step more lively. Box must fidget and fume, no matter how small the infernal stage is. You're standing there with your elbows tucked in. Loosen up — "

80

Eric, a gleam of sweat on his rawboned face, re-treated behind scenes. Seconds ticked off. Brutus had begun to glower when all at once the door flew open, and onto the stage skipped a fat little man with a head as bald as a doorknob.

"Ta de da da!" he shouted, striking a comic pose with one foot in the air.

The whole company started up in a babble of laughter and greeting. Cindy didn't need to be told. Ollie was back!

"Where have you been?" They clustered around him as he jumped down off the stage. "Where'd you come from?"

"Came in through the back door," he said, "and couldn't resist making a proper entrance." Clapping an arm around Maud's shoulders he planted a kiss on her cheek. "There's my gal!" They made a strange couple, she as dry as he was moist and plump.

Trying to hold back a smile she said, "You old rap-scallion, why didn't you write?"

And Brutus had shoved the benches around so they could all sit in a circle. "More to the point, what have you accomplished? When do we open in Denver?"

Ollie seated himself and they settled down around him. Cocking one ankle across the opposite knee he said, with a slight flourish, "Consider this shoe, friends, and grieve for it." It had once been shiney black patent leather, now so scuffed it was beyond polishing. "This bit of innocent leather," he went on with mock sorrow, "has been the victim of more rocks, ruts, ruins, rivers, rime and rough roads than most shoes ever encounter in a lifetime. I've been climbing mountains, scaling cliffs, footing it across precarious precipices and falling into prospect holes. But we're billed — gloriously, lavishly, exultantly billed — all along the gold and silver circuits. Ah yes, friends, that's where the green grows right now." He rubbed two fingers together as if feeling a piece of money.

Cindy felt a little stir of anxiety. He hadn't answered yet about Denver.

"The mountains," he was going on, waving his arms grandly, "these majestic monuments to the west of us are inhabited. They're studded with mine camps, the camps are alive with men, the men starving for entertainment. Golden, Black Hawk, Central City, Georgetown, Idaho Springs, Fairplay — everywhere, I was given a welcome to stir the juices. By the way, Brutus, we must invest in a set of scales. Some of these ragged customers along the streams will have to buy their tickets with gold dust. It's all they've got."

"Are you serious, old man?" Ralph asked wide-eyed.

"Oh, you've got to see it to believe it. Nuggets as big as nuts, chunks of ore all a-glitter with the colors of a peacock. And the men are thirsting for something to spend it on."

"You haven't actually billed us into those outlandish places," Helene demanded.

"Yes, ma'am, that I did. That's my job. That's what we need — audiences, lively ones."

"If they get any livelier than they were in Pueblo, they'll have to be locked in cages," she snapped. "What of the accommodations?"

"You can have your choice of anything, from pestiferous little hotels to pot-luck stage stations. And in the absence of either we carry our own makings for a primitive paradise. Plenty of camp sites up there, friends."

"I did not join this troupe in the role of pioneer mother!" Helene stated sharply. "The understanding was that we would play Denver — or at least some semi-civilized place."

"Well, now, civilization has its drawbacks." Ollie looked around at them ruefully. "Denver is a town of passion, paradox and perspiration. They are having a regular sockdolager of a summer and they're furious over it — not used to such an insult. They tell me the weather's usually salubrious. So they're all a bit mad, and you can't blame them. At an altitude of five thousand feet, the sun feels as if it's positively pounding your pate." He mopped his bald head symbolically.

"You mean it's so hot they've closed the theaters?" Brutus demanded incredulously.

"Hardly. Theaters are all rented up weeks ahead. Months. And there's your paradox. Since the railroad came in last year they're overwhelmed with entertainment of every variety. Place is crawling with Swiss bell ringers and Japanese acrobats, lecturers with anatomical exhibits, lady poetesses — you name it. In the next few weeks, no less than two circuses will be setting up there, a juvenile ballet corps opening, and even those will have a hard time competing with the variety halls. Apparently when it's this hot, your civilized people would rather go to The Cricket and listen to a stage-struck bullwhacker sing 'Mother Kissed Me in My Dream.' Talk to people about the legitimate theater and they go glassy. Even their own resident theatrical company has fled to Wyoming for the rest of the summer."

"But didn't you inform them that we're from New York?" Helene exclaimed.

"Makes no difference, ma'am. Laura Keene, herself, would have to learn to do tightrope tricks to command an audience up there right now. Oh, it's a capricious town of dressy dowagers and princes of the stock market, and Indians whooping it up with horse races along Larimer Street. The fact of the matter is" — he spread his little pink hands helplessly — "I couldn't rent a hall. Until at least next fall, Denver is out."

The talk went on, but Cindy had to get away — to try once more to scrape up the pieces of her ruined plans. How the others could go on and on, being all concerned over such things as what to wear in the mountains and what food they'd need? And her stomach like lead inside her! But then, why should they worry about her problems? It really wasn't any of their business. As quietly as possible, she edged away from the group and went out behind the scenery where she found the rear door open.

Wearily she sank down on the back steps of the hall. Around her the little town lay quiet under the afternoon sun. A neat, prosperous community — no Indians tearing around on their horses. Denver sounded like a wilder place than Pueblo. She hated to think what could happen to a younger type of girl getting off the stagecoach all alone there, even if she had money to buy a ticket.

She tried to figure how much Brutus owed her by now, and when she couldn't, exactly, it made her feel worse. She could almost hear the teacher back in Kansas: "If a person shall have a wage of five dollars per week and only work four days of that week . . ." Cindy never had been able to see much point to all that. Pretty funny now.

For a long time she sat there stricken, with only one image before her eyes — of a lovely woman with a special warmth, a fresh fondness in her smile, all for Cindy. But a long distance off now. It was as if somehow her mother were getting farther and farther away. A hopelessness kept trying to creep in on her, a terrible hunch that they might never find each other again. Trying furiously to shut it out of her mind, Cindy stared off toward the mountains to the north. Sixty miles — you *could* walk that far —

And then someone was coming. Lorna, all a-twitter.

"Oh, there you are, dear! We've been looking for you. Do come in; we're going into dress rehearsal and Durango needs someone to turn pages for him. The music for *Box and Cox* is rather tricky."

He ought to like that, Cindy thought broodingly. And then she knew it wasn't quite fair, for he'd given her no further reason to be suspicious. The more she thought back, the more she had to admit he'd never really done her any harm. And might even have meant it when he'd said he was trying to help.

Not that she trusted him or anything, but right now, she didn't care if she did have to sit with him a while. He was the only one around who wasn't thinking about plays all the time. He'd been through that bad night in Kansas, too. He'd been pretty mad over it himself. And he did seem to know a lot about how to get around places. At least it couldn't hurt to ask him a couple of questions.

He was sitting at the piano, glancing through some sheets of music. Without looking up, he moved to make room for her on the bench beside him. "No wonder these tunes are intricate," he commented, half to himself. "They're by Arthur Sullivan. We'd better run through the score once while the others are changing into costume." Setting the music on the rack he added, "When I nod, please turn the page."

Cindy tried to stay alert, as he began to race through the rapid little melodies of the accompaniment. When he signalled the first time, she turned the page. But then she lapsed into her own troubles and didn't look up again until Durango broke off.

"I guess I know what's on your mind," he said, beginning to finger the keys lightly. "That was bad news for you, just now."

Rousing at the words, Cindy turned to him. "Listen, do you suppose my mother could have gone back to Kansas already to look for me? Lorna said she might."

Durango let his hands rest idle as he turned it over in his mind. Just seeing him consider it, made her feel steadier inside. Some people answer so fast, you know they haven't really thought much.

"I doubt it," he said at last. "Anyway not yet. She'd suppose that you were being taken care of, so she wouldn't be afraid for your safety. And once the Judge assigned you a guardian, before she could get you back she'd probably have to hire a lawyer and put up a court fight. That takes money."

"And we didn't have much. We were only in Kansas a few months, we never could even pay the rent on time. Maybe she doesn't have *any!*" The old fear spurted inside Cindy.

But Durango just went on in that calm tone. "Fortunately, it wouldn't take long to remedy that, in these parts. The miners up in the gold camps will pay handsomely for the pleasure of dancing with a pretty woman. No, I'd say your mother is probably better off right now than you are."

"What makes you think she'd be out in the camps!"

Durango struck a few chords — here and there and there — before he said, "Fact is, Ollie heard something to that effect. I talked with him a few minutes, and he does remember a company of girls arriving in Denver on the train. Didn't pay much attention to the details, but he's fairly sure they were hired on the spot by the proprietor of a dancehall up in one of the mountain towns. Unfortunately he didn't get the name. To him it was only a chance piece of gossip until I inquired."

But now Cindy was suspicious. "Why did you ask him? Why did you care where my mother was? You said you were done with worrying about me."

Durango brought his hands down on the keys with a bang. "I happened to be in pursuit of my own affairs. The manager of that outfit still owes me two weeks' pay."

"Oh." Cindy was taken back a little. Though his face was expressionless, the way he was striking harsh little broken chords — it made her prickle as if she'd insulted somebody and should feel sorry. Maybe he really was just minding his own business. What difference to him, whether she went on to Denver or stayed with the troupe or — anything? She decided to try a secret test.

"What do you think I should do?" she asked, offhand.

"I've no idea. My personal purpose in life is one of self-preservation," he said distantly. "For reasons of my own, I'm stuck with this outfit, like it or not. And I'm not sure I do. These people have no idea of the wild and woolly country they're heading off into. The mountains are full of hazards — the weather, the men, the land itself — all rougher than these gentle actors dream. It's going to try them, in a way they're hardly expecting. They'll be lucky if they don't break up under it. If you do decide to come along, you'd better be thinking about that."

Cindy was watching the people on the stage. They were in costume now, still clustering around Ollie, asking more questions. Even in private conversation they used a lot of little flourishes and manners that they'd borrowed from their play-acting. Handsome as they were, they looked fairly soft, all right.

"But I'm stuck, too," she said. Because if her mother was somewhere in the mountains, Cindy knew she'd never be able to go searching up there alone. She'd better stick with the troupe, even if it was a long chance that they might happen into the right town. "I guess I've got to go along. At least these folks are kind . . ."

"Well, of course, that's up to you. And it's certainly possible their path may cross your mother's, though in the meantime — ? Well, since you're a shade young to be making your own decisions — for what it's worth I'll pass along to you an ancient adage of all vagabonds: When among strangers, consider their motives more carefully than their manners." As he spoke, Durango was beginning to play, some strange personal moody sort of music, his strong fingers moving up and down the keyboard, feeling out patterns. Cindy kept staring at them almost hypnotized, but he hardly seemed aware that he was playing — it was like a part of his thoughts, as he studied the company up on the stage.

"What lies beneath all that finery?" he mused in a low voice. "What reason do you suppose has brought them all out here to a frontier for which they're obviously ill-suited?"

And since Cindy had wondered that herself, already, she didn't mind giving him her own opinion. "It's because they're all afraid to death of Brutus."

"Brutus?" Durango made a little thunder deep down in the base notes of the piano. "Even if you're right — which you may be — what about *him?* What makes him tick, or should I say rumble? Not money, I'll guarantee. And why did the others join him in the first place? Nine of us" — he ran up a flight of sharp chords — "nine people, counting you and me, all prompted by some private reason or other. One on a search. Another in flight; there may be more than one person here escaping from some less inviting fate. And then there's one, at least, who's an utter fool and can't be counted on in the least. That can be a serious consideration, who to turn to in an emergency. Only one of the group, I suspect, has unusual courage. Another, who seemed to have a certain wisdom, I'm beginning to doubt. And one is hopelessly in love, which makes for some instability. The rest — I've not made up my mind — "

Cindy couldn't guess who he might be talking about, but she thought he might be trying to make her suspicious of them all. And for that matter, nobody knew what made Durango tick, as he put it. "They're just people," she said impatiently. "Who cares, anyhow. *Who cares?*"

Durango cocked his head as if that was a good question. "Why, if everything depends on it — your food, clothing, shelter and even your safety — I'd suppose you do."

II

The Factotum

10

THE WAY into the mountains lay straight to the west,
right toward the tallest peak that Cindy had ever seen.
It towered over the hills around it, with forests lying
like a dark shawl across its shoulders and, above timber-
line, only barren rock. It seemed to lean back against
the sky and dare them to pass. She was relieved when
the road swung aside and followed a little stream that
came plunging down out of one of the canyons.

Even going that way, the climb was steep enough. As
the narrow track got rougher they slowed to a turtle's
pace, mile after mile, toiling higher and higher into the
maze of hills. The canyon narrowed down between
wooded slopes that slanted off upward at a dizzy pitch,
leaving only a wedge of sky overhead. And far up on

the heights, Cindy could see huge boulders hanging — sudden stretches of sheer cliff.

It made her a little nervous, but the others seemed marvelously cool. Ollie, back there on the van, sitting beside Brutus on the driver's seat, appeared to be telling funny stories, waving his arms extravagantly. Once in a while his high-pitched laugh would ring on the mountain stillness. Brutus seemed in good spirits too. Only Durango was poker-faced, as always. He had chosen to walk beside the horses, striding along, hands deep in his pockets, head bent.

Probably trying to figure out more about these people, Cindy supposed. These past few days his curious words had kept echoing in her ears as she watched the troupe going about their preparations for the journey. Which one would he think was so brave, or which might be this utter fool? Of course the one in love was easy; Ralph was practically moony over Helene. All day today he'd been showing off on the saddle horse he'd bought himself, cavorting up and down the trail like an idiot.

As for the one "on a search," Cindy knew that had to be her. She had checked with Ollie about the dance hall girls who'd gone off to work in one of the mountain camps, and he'd said it was true. He was even fairly sure the bunch had come from Kansas, so there was nothing to do except go on looking and looking . . . and stick with the troupe.

Stuck. Durango had said it — both of them, stuck.

And that was the biggest question, the one he hadn't wanted to answer the other day. Why should he have to go along with these people who worried him? Maybe he did need money, but then they all said he was such a rare piano player he could get a job anywhere. And yet here he was, tramping up this pass. Cindy had to admit that he really didn't seem to care any more about what she did — telling her to make her own decisions and all. So it wasn't that.

Which left her to suppose that he must have meant himself when he said "one in flight." It brought back a memory of those rumors, how he probably had a price on his head. Cindy wondered what the other women would think if they knew that. Maybe they wouldn't be acting so blithe right now.

Maud had loosened the puckerstring on the back canvas of the wagon and tied the flaps up, so they could all look out. With chairs drawn in a semicircle so close they were knee-to-knee, they sat watching the trail fall away slowly behind them. A cool afternoon breeze was stirring; several times Lorna had pronounced it "delightful." Maud was busy with her crocheting, going at it hammer and tongs, thrusting the hook as vigorously as if she were jabbing an adversary.

Even Helene, who was still skeptical of this journey, was taking it lightly enough now they were on their way. "At least we won't die of thirst." She kept saying gay little things like that. "This is a sweet brook. It has good sense, rushing back toward civilization. Hurry

98

away, little stream, run! Until you find the broad Missouri and then — on to the Mississippi! Off with you!
Tumble on down to New Orleans, rush forth into the
blue ocean. And when you finally mingle with the waters around New York, kiss its sweet shores for me."

"What play did you crib those lines from?" Maud
asked, in a bluff way that was as near teasing as she ever
got.

Helene just laughed. "Go on, Maudie, be cynical. Be
urbane. We must do our best not to become uncouth
out here in this land of whiskery gold-grubbers. I'll
strike my blow for culture — Little Cinders, run get
my manicure set. Quick!"

Cindy was glad enough to oblige. It was one task she
liked. Such delicate, beautiful hands as Helene's — it
was a real privilege to be allowed to buff those slender
nails. Making her way up to the front end of the
wagon, in the dimness she searched for the traveling
bag, found the little leather packet, then paused to lift
the front curtain a minute.

On the driver's seat, Eric was absorbed in one of the
plays — didn't even look up. There was nothing ahead
anyhow but more of the twisting track, the canyon and
deep woods on either side. Going back to the women,
Cindy settled herself on the footstool beside Helene.

She could certainly see why all this was pretty uncouth for someone from a handsome eastern city. She'd
heard about those places; they were where all the most
important people lived. As she took Helene's hand and

began carefully to polish the long, pink, perfect nails, she asked, "What's it like in New York?"

A distant look of remembered pleasure quickened Helene's eyes and her eyebrow raised a fraction. "It's handsome men and walks in the park and music halls and dinner at Delmonico's. It's Wall Street and Broadway and the dear old Hudson, and flowers in the dooryard of Trinity Church on Easter. It's heaven!"

"With a bit of the other place thrown in," Maud added. "Tenements, beggars, long lines of hungry people out of work."

"It can be a very difficult city," Lorna nodded wistfully. "We should just be thankful we're with a troupe, practicing our profession even in the wilderness."

Helene was shaking her head. "I'll be blistered if I count it such good fortune. To poke along behind these dreary nags, instead of racing on the concourse with a handsome pair of trotters."

"Did you have your own horses?" Cindy marvelled.

"She's borrowing from the playwrights again," Maud sniffed.

"Don't listen to her, Little Cinders. I owned the most beautiful imaginary horses — and what's wrong with that? There's more than one way to win a race! When I finished that scene, I had the audience on its feet, cheering."

All at once Helene sat up straighter in her seat, her face taking on a sudden warmth, her voice thrilling in that way it did when she was acting a part: "*You ought* to have seen those ponies throw out their dear little feet. When we came up to Fastboy he wanted to pull up—too much of a gentleman, you know, to race with a lady. But his horses didn't share his feelings in that respect and nearly pulled him over the dasher, so he let them go and away we went, like twin bullets, neck and neck!"

In the prettiest way, Helene pretended to be holding a pair of reins, leaning forward a little breathless, her eyes shining. "I kept my arms down and had the ponies well together so everything turned aside for us — we had a clear road for a mile. I couldn't hear anything but the rattling of the wheels and the tip tip of the ponies' hoofs. My heart beat like a steam engine, it was clear up in my mouth. And I beat him, I beat him, I beat him!"

For a minute Cindy could almost feel the rush of wind in her face and see the surging finish. Then Lorna applauded and the spell was broken.

"Nicely done, Helene," she said. "I didn't know you'd ever played the leading role in *Young New York.*"

"Oh yes, she played it once," Maud nodded, "when the regular lead was ill. The rest of the time, she was the secondary, weren't you, dear?"

Helene stood up as if she were a bit put out. Even jumpy for some reason. Wandering toward the front of the wagon she said restlessly, "I wonder if that boy can't get a little more speed out of those ancient plugs. He's probably afraid to give them a touch of the whip." She lifted the curtain, started to let it fall, then paused, staring out front as if she were startled. "No wonder we're going so slow. That left horse is limping."

Maud dropped the crochetwork and hurried to her side. She called out, "Eric! Pull up! Angels and ministers of grace, can't you see you've got a lame horse?"

"You foolish boy," Helene scolded in a brittle, high voice, "with your nose stuck in that book — "

Lorna simply sat there rigid, staring at Cindy. "I knew it, I knew we'd get stranded in some God-forsaken spot." She folded her hands as if she were prepared to die a slow death.

Cindy was puzzled, because a lame horse was no terrible great shucks, and besides, they had plenty of food along. Only a day's hike back to town. Suddenly she realized that if they could come a-fluster so easily it must be because they had been fearful all along. They were still dithering when the men came up.

Ollie hopped around, helping Eric unharness, while Brutus stood bristling. The heavy hair seemed to spring backward from his boney forehead more furiously than usual — stiff as a lion's mane — as he considered the weary roan. It stood hipshot in the midst of the excitement, one foot cocked gingerly.

"Well, well!" Ollie tried to sound cheerful. "A drama critic once said I should have been a blacksmith . . ."

"Where's Ralph?" Helene asked irritably. But he'd

ridden on ahead. Cindy figured it must have been two hours or more since they'd last seen him.

Brutus bent down to examine the horse's hoof, but the awkward way he took hold of it showed that he was no hand with animals. Straightening, he eyed the old roan as if he wished he could hurl a few Green Room rules at it. Cindy could picture it: Article 27 — Any plug that goes lame without notice —

Then as if Eric were a more likely subject, he swung around and confronted the boy. "Well, sir, how long has it been favoring that foot?"

"I can't — be sure. I was studying my lines," Eric stammered.

"Shades of eternal glory! Don't you realize that these beasts are our sole means of locomotion?"

Red-faced and apologetic, the boy fell mute. From the jut of his elbows and sloping shoulders, Cindy knew how he felt. She always came all loose inside when a teacher would call her on the carpet in front of everybody. It just makes you act that much stupider. She was glad when they heard hoofbeats and Ralph galloped up.

"Halloo," he called. "I thought you'd be farther along than this. Only a few miles ahead the trail levels out, going's much easier. I've been — scouting the way." Which didn't explain why his boots were all muddy, Cindy noticed. But the others didn't question him about it; they were too busy telling him of their misfortune.

"Well, let's just take a look," he said in a business-like way, stepping over to the roan. Picking up the sore hoof, he probed with his fingers. "I'd say he's bruised his foot on a stone as we came along."

Brutus nodded impatiently. "I thought of that. But what to do about it?"

"Simple." Ralph brushed off his hands. "The fellow who sold me the mare also provided me with an excellent preparation guaranteed to cure all ailments of horses, a sort of liniment, I think. Smells vile — must be good. By tomorrow this nag will be frisky as a colt."

But Brutus seemed to doubt it. Glancing around, he located Durango. The piano player stood a short distance apart from them as if he hardly thought it was any of his business. And yet Brutus addressed him now with sudden inspiration.

"You, sir. I'll wager you've had some experience of your own with such matters. Would you care to give us an opinion?"

Durango came over slowly, picked up the horse's hoof — it only took a glance and he said, "Opinions are chancey. Facts are another matter. This is a poor shoeing job; the hoof's beginning to split. This horse isn't going to be hauling a wagon tomorrow."

They stood staring at each other aghast. "And we're billed to open in Fairplay on Saturday!"

Brutus nodded grimly. "If only we'd noticed the trouble before we came so far from town — " He broke off, but they all looked at Eric.

Durango turned to the boy, too. "You probably carry a clawhammer in your carpentry box?"

Eric took the chance to escape, hurrying off to the van where they kept the tools for building scenery.

"Ah, then you think you can remedy the situation?" Brutus asked hopefully.

"No, but the shoe's got to be taken off if the horse is going to keep up with us tomorrow," Durango explained. "I assume you don't want to abandon it."

"Go? *How*, man?" Ollie, Brutus — all of them hung on the answer to that.

Durango looked surprised. "You've still got six horses."

"By George, if you're referring to my mare," Ralph blustered, "I'll have you know that tender little creature has never felt the pangs of harness and — "

"Oh yes, she has," Durango nodded carelessly. "Those are strap marks on her chest and withers. She's a sturdy little mustang, no temperament about her. She'll pull if she's made to."

"A good motto for this entire company to observe." Brutus gave Ralph a look that meant if there weren't a Green Room rule to cover the situation he'd make one up. Eric had come back with the hammer now and they set to work prying the crooked shoe off, while Ralph paced back and forth, slapping his boot with the little crop he carried.

"Fortunate thing, to be a jack-of-all-trades," he remarked acidly. "Watch sharp, Eric, and if you don't make a vet, perhaps you'll discover how to play the piano."

Haggard with embarrassment the boy shut his lips in a tight, painful line.

"What this lad must learn — " Brutus was beginning, direly, when he was cut shot by a sound. Down off the heights it came, a yelping that rose to a long thin scream.

"A wolf!" Lorna gasped.

"A whole pack of them!" Maud muttered. For there followed a whole chorus of sharp, ragged yelps, rising in a pitch of excitement until they shrieked like the laughter of a crew of demons up there on the crags. The sun had gone behind the hills, blue shadows pouring down the long slopes in a darkening tide. For a minute the whole company stood transfixed, listening. The sudden silence that followed was almost worse than the eerie noise.

Ralph got out a small pearl-handled pistol and brandished it. "Don't worry, ladies. I am armed!"

Hunkered down on his heels, working on the shoe, Durango glanced up at the actor sharply. Brutus caught the direction of the look and seemed to take some hint from it.

"Ralph," he said curtly, "put that thing away before you shoot one of us. You can render yourself more useful by collecting firewood. We'd best be about the business of making camp — darkness is descending."

"I insist that Ralph stand guard against those

wolves," Helene spoke up with a quaver. "At least the first watch. We must all take turns to keep the fire going. It's well known that the fiendish beasts surround their victims and steal in through the dark . . ." The others began to glance around uneasily.

Durango straightened with the shoe in his hand. "You're more or less right about wolves. If they're hungry enough, they'll bother you. But those coyotes up there are shy little varmints who hardly ever aspire much higher than a jackrabbit to satisfy their appetites."

"Speaking of that," Ollie put in, "let's get the cookery going, ladies." For the women were still inclined to dither, and Ralph continued to toy with the gun.

"Yes, and the teams must be unhitched," Brutus added, turning once more to Eric. "As for you, young man — well, what *can* we give you to do, eh?"

Without seeming to direct the remark at anyone, Durango said, "Somebody's got to take care of this unfortunate, harassed animal. It's been doing its job the best it could all day under difficulties; its nerves are in bad shape. It deserves pasture and quiet, I'd say, if it's to feel up to taking the road again tomorrow and eventually see more useful service. I suggest it be led back — slowly — to that little glade we passed a hundred yards or so down the trail and staked out for the night."

Brutus seemed puzzled, but it was plain he was beginning to respect Durango's knowledge of horses. "Do it, then," he told Eric. "Make the beast comfortable."

As the boy led the roan away, the others scattered to the tasks set for them. But Cindy kept wondering, whenever her glance strayed to Durango. He was helping the other men unhitch the rest of the teams, going about his work as soberly as if he hadn't played an odd joke on them just now — for whatever reason. Because if there was ever a horse without nerves, Cindy thought, it was the roan.

I I

MORE AND MORE Cindy wondered about this unfathomable man. Durango. This liar. But she thought it a little more kindly just now, as she sat beside him on the driver's box of the covered wagon. Even if he had made her believe once that he wanted nothing to do with guns, she was just as glad he really knew how to handle the rifle that lay across his knees.

Yesterday he had bagged a fine supper for the whole company. After nearly a week on the road they had all got tired of jerked beef and dried fruit. Ralph had been trying to bring down some game, but the deer were too fast and the antelope too wary. The fact was, he simply was no shot.

So Durango had borrowed his rifle and, after a

couple of practice rounds, had brought down a half-dozen young grouse as they had traveled along during the day. The easy way he swung the gun to his shoulder when the birds rose, sometimes dropping two out of the same covey, Cindy thought it must have taken years to learn to shoot like that.

And to know horses as he did! Ever since they had put the mare in harness with the larger dray horse, Durango had driven the mismatched team, and though they had moved slowly, no more injuries had developed. He chose a pace that wouldn't overtax the animals and called frequent halts, to let them rest, no matter how the other members of the troupe fretted at the delay.

They were far behind schedule, of course. And so today Brutus had decided to carry on a rehearsal right there in the back of the covered wagon. It meant that Cindy had to sit out on the box to make room. Not that she minded. Durango had an odd way of making her feel welcome around him, even if his talk was curious.

But today they had ridden in silence, mile after mile. Beneath the brim of the dark hat his eyes were on the move constantly, scanning the whole breadth of this new world they had come into.

A vast tableland thousands of feet higher than the plains they'd left behind, it was deep in the tallest grass that Cindy had ever seen. Walled in by jagged peaks so high they were still patched with heavy snowdrifts. Yet here on the flat it was hot. In fact the sun did seem, as

Ollie declared, to beat down harder in the thin air. Though it was still June, the wild hay was yellowing, and swarms of grasshoppers burst upward from the track as the wagons moved slowly along.

They were following a new stream toward those western mountains — that's where the mine camps were. What breed of man might live so far from anywhere, Cindy could only guess. She wondered if Durango knew. But even though he was always on the watch, his head was tilted slightly as if he were also listening to the sounds of the rehearsal coming from the rear of the wagon.

Eric, speaking his lines with dogged determination: "*Oh, my dear Mary, I hove down as fast as I could make sail, bless your dear toplights* — " He broke off. "What are 'toplights' anyhow?"

"A nautical reference to her eyes," Brutus' voice came impatiently. "Try the speech again — make it reek of salt. A sailor returned from the sea has a personal rhythm like an ocean swell."

But the boy was getting jerkier all the time. He would sort of burst out with the words in little bunches: "*After fighting the — the — briny b-b-billows* — "

Brutus swore angrily. "Confound it! Still stuttering your *b*'s. That's a lack of concentration, sir."

And Helene's voice rose, high and fraught with nerves. "If he takes me in his arms and says '*B-b-bless your dear toplights*' like that, I shall probably have hysterics — I warn you!"

"Brutus" — that was Lorna's gentle tone — "may I be excused for a while. I — I really feel quite dizzy."

"Excused? Shall we all be excused then? Leave it to pure chance — the whim of fate — whether our performance falters tomorrow night?" Brutus seemed to make an effort at patience. "Come, we must go through these parts thoroughly. We've not even looked at this play since we performed it in Dodge City, and then the roles were assigned differently, thanks to the late, unlamented Peter."

That was what the rehearsal was all about — Eric moving up to take his first major role, and Lorna assigned to play the bit part he used to do. Only a few lines, but it was upsetting her. She'd never dressed like a man in her life. Cindy couldn't see why she was so undone over it, and it really was a good chance for Eric. Even though he only came in once at the beginning and once at the end, it meant everything to the play.

A story about a mean man who had come home after twenty years and was going to get revenge on his brother, by turning him out of the family home and sending him to jail. And the only thing that saved the poor, good brother was his daughter, who was going to marry this handsome young sailor — Eric's role — who came home and in the last act talked the mean brother out of being so mean. Nobody even died at the end.

In fact it was a fairly funny play in places, because

Ollie and Maud were "Mr. and Mrs. Toodles," and they kept coming on between the serious scenes and having comical arguments, fussing and squabbling. They were the best part of the show. Right now they were back there driving the van, rehearsing their parts as they went along. Glancing back, Cindy wished she could hear what they were saying. She could see them shaking their fists at each other and raving. Of all the people in the troupe, they were the only ones who didn't seem to get more and more upset these days of traveling farther up into the wild country.

Right now Lorna sounded as if she were going to pieces; she was almost crying. "I can't do it, Brutus. I've never played a male part — I don't think I'm right for it. Oh — I feel faint — "

Cindy glanced at Durango. "I guess maybe they're all sort of utter fools," she admitted ruefully.

He just looked worried. "There's nothing temperamental about coming down with mountain sickness."

"You mean Lorna's really got something?"

"I'd say she's feeling the altitude. It's laid many a person low for the first week or so. I wonder if Brutus knows that."

"He's been so worked up himself, ever since that silly business about the horse going lame — "

Durango shook his head. "Nothing silly about that, either. It could have spelled disaster. For a man like Brutus, his greatest pride is to honor his commitments and present a first-class play on the day he's promised

to. A matter of self respect as well as funds."

"I figured they must be short of money," Cindy agreed thoughtfully. "Because Helene's mad. They haven't been paid since Pueblo. Neither have I, but she's a great *actérienne*, even if she has been having flutters ever since she mistook those coyotes for wolves." Cindy chuckled a little. It had pleased her to find there was at least one thing she knew more about than Helene. "When she said, 'We must all stand guard — ' "

But Durango didn't laugh. "No way for her to know they weren't wolves. And if they had been — " Squinting against the bright glare of the day he seemed to be seeing something that happened a long time ago. "I can remember sitting up all night myself, feeding a fire, with a pack of those gray devils ringed around me. It's no delusion — you can see their eyes glint in the dark."

Cindy lapsed into a chagrined silence. She had thought those stories were just tales the cowboys concocted to scare her. Now — to picture Durango out alone in some desolate spot, just a little handful of fire to drive back the deep darkness, and hungry things prowling just beyond — she could envision the whole thing just in the quiet distance of his eyes. Then she saw his look sharpen slightly, as if he'd spotted something.

For a minute she couldn't see any sign of life in all that waving grassland. Then she made out the far-off buff and white of an antelope herd, bobbing away, light as fluff. A red-tailed hawk swooped out there, lost in the deep growth, then rising again to soar away down the wind with a varmint kicking in its claws. All this . . . but Durango saw something more. Cindy looked again and sat up straighter.

A lonely shabby figure hunched over on the stream bank, almost the same gray as the pile of rock behind him. It seemed incredible to find a man out here in the middle of nowhere, afoot. As they came closer they could see that he was working a broad, flat pan, sluicing water in and out, thumbing over the gravel in the bottom of it. From the tall grass nearby a burro raised its head and let out a long raw-edged heehaw.

The mare whickered back and the fellow looked up. Jumping to his feet he stood staring, then set the pan down and came running toward the road.

"Gol-durned dang-slatted son-of-a-sourdough, if you ain't the actor people!" he whooped as they came up. "We been watchin' for you all week!"

Durango touched his hat. "How far are we from Fairplay, friend? Will we get there by sundown?"

"Bust my long-johns if it ain't gonna be a treat — to get played at by real, livin' kickin' actors. Is that Millie up there on the box with you?" He peered up, trying to see past Cindy's sunbonnet. Durango looked at her, puzzled.

She whispered, "Helene — that's who he means."

Durango still looked perplexed. "No, Miss Paree is inside right now, resting."

116

"Well, tell her to rest good and bust the slats out of us tomorrow night. 'Cause we'll all be there sure. No, I ain't gonna tell you how far 'tis, you might change your mind and not try to make it tonight. And there's a bunch more fellers waitin' there to get a look at you. Just keep a-goin' — " He waved them grandly ahead.

As the wagon rolled on, Cindy turned to find that the rest of the troupe had crowded up to the front curtain, listening.

"That man was panning for gold!" Ralph told them excitedly. "Did you see his pan? I wonder if he's found any. The South Platte is supposed to be pretty rich, I've heard. Maybe we should — I mean couldn't the horses use a bit of rest?"

Durango shook his head. "I've an idea we'd better keep going if you want to reach town by dark."

"Correct!" Brutus agreed emphatically. "There's no time for such frivolity if we're to earn our more particular fortunes at the box office tomorrow night." The flap fell, and Durango and Cindy were alone again under the brassy dome of the sky.

He seemed to be musing over something. "Millie . . . ?"

"Well — you know — the posters," Cindy said. "They all read: 'Mlle. Paree'. I didn't know what it meant either until she told me it was French, and she gets called that because it means 'Miss' over in Europe, where she de-rives from."

Durango's taut face broke abruptly into a swift laugh

that was so good-humored it startled Cindy. "Derives, indeed. About three generations back. Underneath the stage manner, that accent of hers is pure Hoboken. Her real name is probably Helen Perkins."

"Where's Hoboken?" Cindy felt a little uncomfortable, as if maybe she'd been naïve. It irritated her, to think Helene could have considered her so gullible. "Anyhow, if she did change her name — a lot of people do that." Nobody on earth was ever really named Durango, she thought darkly.

He got the unspoken accusation and grew sober again, his face unreadable as ever. "Have you ever thought about it? Changing your name?" And the slight taunting mockery was back again.

"I wish it wasn't Ferris," she retorted, before she thought. Never had intended to tell him anything so personal, but since she'd started, she had to go on. "I hate my father. I don't even want his name on me!"

Durango swung the loose end of the reins to smash a horsefly on the mare's crupper, so skillfully she hardly blinked. "Fathers . . ." he began distantly and even the mockery was gone. As he seemed about to go on, from inside the wagon they could hear Eric stammering his lines, Brutus making explosive noises.

"Poor Eric," Cindy said fervently.

"If you think he's poor," Durango suggested, "why don't you help him?"

"Me? How?"

"That's something only you could decide — women

118

have an intuition about such things. And a marvelous sympathy."

"Well, I'd tell him first not to be so scared of Brutus, it's getting him all strung up. And that's what I mean about fathers." So go ahead and give me a lecture on how sinful it is to say things against your own father, she invited him silently.

But Durango's eyes had taken on a gleam like new ice. "When it comes to that, I've had some experience, myself," he said. "My father — was the reason I once found myself in the company of wolves." And from the way he shut his lips, she knew that it was all he was going to say.

12

From the main road a single track led toward the wild peaks, and at the lower edge of the foothills stood a cluster of cabins and shacks and stables. Fairplay was so much the same roughness as the outcroppings of timber around, it was as if the whole town had sprung up out of the earth by some natural force. At the far end of the single rutted road through the camp stood the largest and newest of the buildings, the logs still bleeding sap. And it was from the wall of this one that the theater bill blazed, in all its vibrant gold and red lettering:

BRUTUS BRAITHWAITE'S THESPIANS

Presenting

"THE TOODLES"

A Domestic Drama in Two Acts

to be followed by

"BOX AND COX"

A side-splitting,
Vest-popping,
Button-shooting Farce

The poster also was decorated with a large picture of a woman down on her knees with her hands clasped. She didn't look much like Helene, but underneath were the words "Mlle. Paree as Mary" and a quotation from the play:

"He would not — could not — be so cruel!
My tears should pierce his heart!"

It was absolutely beautiful, Cindy thought, as she stood before it in the pale light of early morning.

The other women were still asleep, so she'd slipped out alone to look at the town. It had been too late to see much of it when they got in last night. But it seemed like a lively place, from the crowd of people that turned out to meet them. The same kind of men they'd passed all yesterday afternoon along the stream — boisterous fellows who yelled and waved their hats.

Surrounding the wagons, a whole horde of them had escorted the troupe to its sleeping quarters — some attic rooms up over an eating house. Cindy personally thought it was a pretty wild one. All night long the gaiety kept exploding downstairs, while in the rooms above, the shivering women lay in bed and listened to the crash of broken glass, the rumble of heavy laughter.

Once there was a snarling argument and a burst of gunfire.

To Cindy it brought back all the dread she used to feel, off there in Kansas when the trail crews came to town. But these men were a lot tougher. So long out here alone in the mountains, they sounded like some sort of lusty animals. She had finally gone to sleep to the racket of their voices and was surprised to waken at dawn and find everything quiet.

And now, to venture forth and discover the town almost empty — Where had they all disappeared to? She looked toward the mighty crests to the west — the Continental Divide someone said it was, the high backbone of the whole country. She supposed the miners must be up there in the forests, sleeping. But they would be down again tonight; they had all roared their promises to be at the show.

Standing before the big windowless log building, she felt a rankling uneasiness at the thought of being cooped in there with a whole lot of rough people. It obviously had never been meant for a theater, only a single narrow door in front. She hoped there was some way to get out through the rear of the place, and went on around to make sure.

Eric was back there, already at work unloading scenery from the wagons which were drawn up behind the building. At sight of her he nodded, but he didn't look too-happy. She was reminded of her task. She was going to do something for this poor fellow. Not just because Durango had suggested it — but she understood so well the kind of trap he must be in. She'd felt it too often herself — badgered by older people, like the sheriff, forced to do things their way, obey their orders. Eric needed help, all right.

Climbing up into the rear of the van, Cindy began to hand things down to him — the cardboard tombstones for the graveyard scene, the paper bushes and tulips for the garden setting.

"At least it won't be hard to rig a curtain in there," Eric said as he hauled out the long heavy role of canvas. "Let's pray that I can make it work smoothly."

Gathering up the ropes and pulleys Cindy followed him inside. It took her a minute to adjust to the dimness. From the heavy beams overhead, lanterns hung. Eric had lighted several; their smoke eddied up toward a single vent in the middle of the roof and they spread a pallid circle of light. She could just make out the crude benches that had been set up — bare boards supported by big rounds cut from logs. In close-set ranks they covered the bare earthen floor.

The only part of the building that had a wooden base was a raised platform at the rear end. It was made of huge timbers, as if to take some weighty load, and though it was useful as a stage, Cindy thought it must have been meant for something more than that. There was already a hulking piece of machinery in place over

to one side. Couldn't make out what it was . . .

But Eric was laying out the curtain now; she went to help. Together they spread it on the floor, a big square of canvas with a painting on it of angels flying around with trumpets and harps.

As the boy began to thread the ropes through the loops he seemed to be practicing his lines to himself. "The blue brook bubbled below the black boulder . . . the blue brook . . ."

"Is that in the play!" Cindy asked, dumfounded.

"It's an exercise, supposed to make me quit stumbling over my *b*'s. Ollie composed it for my b-b-b" — he snapped his fingers — "benefit. Holy salvation, if I do that in front of the audience tonight — "

Cindy looked out at the cavernous big room, trying to picture the place full of that noisy rabble which had greeted them yesterday. She'd never worried much about the audience. Most of the time when she was behind the scenes she was hardly aware of them, though when she did Little William she felt them out there, approving. Clapping, to thank her for doing such a good job.

"Listen," she said, "couldn't you die somewhere at the end of the play? They really like that sort of thing."

Eric gave her a bleak smile. "If I died in the first act it would b-be b-b-better." He shook his head in exasperation. "That exercise isn't helping a b-bit. I tried to tell Father it's something else, it isn't just my tongue getting clumsy. But he says I'm not concentrating — only I am. I am . . ." His voice petered out in a mutter of perplexity.

It just made Cindy all the more certain; Brutus was scaring him out of his wits. Earnestly she said, "They don't always know best — none of them do. They mostly want to show you they're boss. You can't let them bully you."

Eric roused out of his own thoughts. "Who? Who are you talking about?"

"Well, you know — grown-ups."

For a minute he stared at her, baffled. "That's an odd thing to say. But then I guess it's b-because you haven't started thinking of yourself as one yet." And he went on threading the ropes, leaving Cindy to feel as if somehow she'd made a slight fool of herself. As he rigged the pulleys he kept mumbling along. "It's that line — 'After fighting the b-briney billows' — if I could just say it fast enough. Without thinking about it . . ."

But Brutus always told everybody to round off each word, even the periods. He was after Eric constantly to say this or that a little differently, lift one shoulder higher or turn his head a fraction. It was making the boy get stiffer by the minute. Cindy wondered what she could do about it.

Wandering around the gloomy building, she had come to the piece of machinery, a mean-looking contraption with wheels and chutes and clawlike things, and some heavy iron parts that resembled giant potato mashers. "Whatever do you reckon that's for?" she wondered absently.

Eric came over to stand beside her, looking at it, too, with an air of perplexity. "Durango says it's a stamp mill; this building is going to be used for milling ore. Those things are crushers."

Surprised, Cindy asked, "When did he tell you that?"

"He was around early this morning." Eric sounded almost irritated. "He's always turning up, making a lot of smart remarks."

"What sort of remarks?" Cindy thought Durango hardly said a word to the troupe as a rule.

"Well, he asks these questions — not really questions — I mean it gets you puzzled. Those double-edged things he says — "

"Like what?"

"Oh, just like — I don't know. Some kinds of ore — pounding them to bits just makes little rocks out of big rocks. What in tarnation was he hinting about? Of course, I know. I know what he meant, all right. He thinks I'm getting choppy, and maybe I am. But what does he expect me to do?" The boy shrugged angrily. "Maybe go off to a nice deserted spot again, in company of an ancient nag, and turn myself into an actor? Not that I couldn't — I think I could — but it would be stupid, to give up the chance to learn from a man like my father. Even if he does — Well, I just told Durango, I put him straight. Anybody — I mean any kind of rough ore needs refining." And he turned away restlessly, to go back to his work.

Cindy wasn't too sure what Eric had meant, with his disjointed harangue, but she knew one thing. He hadn't bumbled his *b*'s once when he was so hot about Durango. So maybe it was good for him to argue. Maybe — her intuition suggested — maybe if she could get him into a really good squabble it would brace him up even more.

There was no chance to try it that afternoon, though. Everything was in a confusion. The troupe had to work fast, to get the props out, the scenery set up. Snatching quick bites of cold food, they rehearsed right on up to curtain time that evening. At last they all went off to the dressing rooms, which were just two curtained-off corners of the building, and began to put on their grease paint. All except Ollie; he was out at the front door selling tickets to a clamorous mob.

They were pouring into the theater. It sounded like thousands of them, jostling the benches around, getting seated, with a husky clamor of talk. Cindy felt some misgivings at the sound of that hubbub, but Brutus looked pleased. And when Ollie finally hurried backstage, he was carrying a heavy canvas bag that chinked.

"The house is full to the last inch and so's this" — he handed Brutus the money bag — "and this!" A little leather pouch — he tossed it in the air. "Gold dust!"

Ralph got bug-eyed at the words, but Helene seemed nervous, even irritated. "They sound like a den of bears out there."

"Had to lock the doors," Ollie nodded, "or we'd have had a stampede." He hurried off to change into his costume, and the others began to take their places in the wings, ready for their entrances.

Over to the left of the stage Eric waited, alone. As Cindy saw him there, standing tensely, she thought she saw her chance, and strolled over to join him. He was repeating the exercise in a hoarse whisper. "The blue brook babbled . . ."

"Watch out you don't say that tonight when you're on," she said brashly. And it worked. He lost that intent frown and gave her a dirty look.

"Don't put such an idea in my mind, for the love of heaven!"

Pleased, Cindy thought if he could just swing out with all his sentences like that, he'd be all right. Still in that teasing tone she said, "Don't be so nervous. This isn't the only job in the world. You don't know it, but I've been a lot of places and seen plenty of jobs" — no point mentioning they were her mother's — "and you just can't let people bother you. That's what I meant this morning. I shouldn't have said 'grown-ups,' that was a baby thing to say. What I meant was people. Everybody! You just have to ignore them. They pick on you, they make you work and work, and they tell you you're not concentrating and all that — "

A hard hand fell on Cindy's shoulder and she jumped. It was Brutus in a ferocious beard and terrible dark eye-paint. He was the mean brother in the play, the villain. Standing over her he said ominously, "Young lady, what is your particular assignment to-night?"

"I haven't got one," Cindy admitted.

"Then I suggest you make yourself useful as an ornament, a conversation piece — a curiosity, if you don't mind. Kindly go out front and sit with Durango. Regale the audience with smiles — anything — but go."

Somewhat abashed, Cindy went. And yet as she was about to step out between the side curtains, she hesitated. The place was packed with men, scrambling around on the benches, trying to make room for one more to squeeze in. On all sides they stood, clear back into the farthest corners. Taking a deep breath, Cindy stepped out into view, caught in the glow of the candles which were already burning in their reflectors across the front of the stage.

At sight of her the men let out a yell, but she hurried quickly down to the shelter of the piano bench, where Durango sat, beginning to feel out his first chords. He looked at her curiously, so she had to explain.

"Brutus told me to stay out here. He's sneaking around back there, making everybody nervous. I tried to help Eric, but there wasn't time. He's all upset."

Durango just struck up a good brisk tune, and again the crowd clapped. They were making an awful lot of

130

noise, much worse than the mule skinners in Pueblo —
gabbing, cracking jokes. Cindy felt as if they were almost breathing down her neck, they were packed so
close up to the stage.

"That feller plays a dandy piano, don't he?"

"Been a long time since I heard a good old agony-
box."

"Purty little gal settin' there. Reckon she's gonna
sing?"

"It ain't called for on the show bill."

"Well, they didn't mention they had a piano feller,
either. Say, you know, I seen him somewhere before."

Durango's fingers didn't miss a note, but Cindy
sensed that he had stiffened, instantly. Began to play a
little faster, a new tune that set them to tapping their
feet. Somebody began to sing along with it.

". . . bet my money on a bob-tail nag, somebody
bet on the bay."

"Yes, sirree," the voice behind them went on. "I
know that feller." A hand reached forward to pluck at
Durango's sleeve. "Say, buster, was you ever down
Santa Fe way?"

He shook his head without turning.. "Afraid you've
got the wrong man, friend." But Cindy had never seen
his fingers move so fast, ripping off the music in a fury
now.

"Well, he sure reminds me of a feller used to bum
around Santa Fe, bird by the name of Paul Dexter — "

And Cindy saw Durango's eyes flicker at the name.

But before the man could say more, the mutter of talk began to quiet. A bell had been struck somewhere backstage — once, twice. It was the way Brutus always announced that the play was ready to begin. Some of the men in the audience stood up and turned down the lanterns that swung overhead, leaving only the stage aglow with light. The canvas curtain with its angels began to quiver; then slowly — in short jogs — it went up.

13

THE OPENING SCENE of the play was in a garden. Somehow the candlelight seemed almost to transform the paper bushes into real shrubbery, and the landscape on the backdrop looked as if it did stretch off to a blue seashore. Even though Cindy herself had helped set it up, she was captivated by the sudden illusion of a dooryard on a sunny day. Around her the audience, too, was in a hush as Helene came on, pausing gracefully to glance around.

"Oh, how beautiful is this morning . . ." As she began to speak, a sigh went through the close-crowded miners, a rustling as if they were stirred by a current of emotion. Durango's fingers touched the piano keys so

lightly, only the faintest thread of music accompanied her words. "... *this day that I'm to be united to my dear Charles.*"

That was Eric's cue. He strode on stage, affecting the rolling gait of a seaman. In the sailor's jacket and hat, he looked fairly tarry, but his voice was strained; he was speaking too carefully as he said: "*Oh, my dear Mary, I hove down as fast as I could make sail, bless your dear toplights . . .*"

And from the first row one of the miners muttered, "He ain't enough of a man for her. Look how timid he grabbed hold of her."

Cindy wriggled, wishing she were near enough to kick him. But now Ralph had made his entrance, all wigged and bearded to look like an old man. He was playing the good brother, Mary's father, telling a long, sad story of how her mother had died when she was a baby. To Eric, he finally said: "*I commit, to thy keeping, the dearest treasure of my heart.*"

In the audience, the same miner spoke up abruptly. "I wouldn't do it. The boy looks too dang young to me." He said it right out loud and the actors on stage gave a startled glance in that direction. Cindy turned to glare at the man, but the other fellows were nodding seriously, as if they agreed.

Intently Ralph went on with his speech: "*Be thou to her what her father has been and I shall die contented.*" And Durango let go with a rousing good string of chords, like church bells ringing.

134

It was the cue for Lorna to make her appearance as an old farmer. Leaning on a cane, she limped across the stage, her slender womanly figure enveloped in a heavy overcoat, straw hat, boots, wig, beard and spectacles. In a creaky voice she began: *"I'm sorry to be the bearer of unpleasant news. Old Nipcheese, the purser, sent me . . ."* She faltered and broke off.

Eric kept watching her nervously as he said: *"Why, what's in the wind now, Farmer? No ill storm b-brewing, I hope?"*

But her voice was thin as she spoke her lines, telling him of his orders to go back on board his ship.

Eric took a deep breath. Rapidly he said: *"This is too bad! After biting the finey brillows for three years —"* He stopped, aghast. Helene turned away, with her back to the audience. Her shoulders were shaking. At last he finished lamely: *" — to be driven out to sea again."*

But now Helene was clinging to Ralph, making muffled sobbing noises. Cindy thought it sounded like hysterics, but the audience took it seriously.

"See, he's already gone and made her cry."

"Well, it wasn't his fault," another argued. "You heard the old man tell him, he's got orders to go back to his ship."

"Oh-oh, look there!"

The strange, muffled figure of the farmer was, in fact, beginning to sag. With a soft thud it collapsed onto the floor like a heap of old clothes. Cindy started

up in spite of herself, but Durango pulled her back, without ever missing a beat in the music. He was playing a little louder now, as the people on the stage bent over Lorna in dismay.

"Well," someone down front remarked solemnly, "that feller's done for, and I'm sorry. I hate to see an old-timer go."

At that moment the curtain came down with a crash that left the angels in the picture all a-shiver. The audience looked a little startled, but they burst out with good, vigorous applause.

One man nudged another, grinning. "Blame good story."

"Sure is plenty goin' on. I like a story with action in it, I swear I do!"

As they subsided into a discussion of just why the old farmer-fellow had "gone up," each advancing some different theory — bad heart maybe, hurried too fast with the message — Cindy sat in sheer disgust.

"They don't even know that they just ruined everything," she muttered.

But Durango, who was pounding out a brisk rendition of "Sail Away Ladies," seemed to be figuring something. "It's not lost, if Brutus wants to go on with it. He could ad-lib to cover Lorna's lines — she didn't have many. I wonder if he realizes how thoroughly the audience is still with him." He glanced at Cindy. "Run backstage and tell him exactly what they're saying. Tell him the old farmer must stay 'dead,' but otherwise — well, just tell him that. Quick now!"

Still sore and confused, Cindy climbed up onto the stage again. The men applauded and whistled, and a fresh surge of indignation went through her. Rushing between the side curtains she ran headlong into Brutus.

"Well, child? What's the tally out there? How did they take that little fiasco of ours?"

As she told him he listened narrowly. Ollie had come up, too. "We'd better not chance it, Brutus — try to go on, with the whole company on the verge of nervous collapse?"

But Brutus' gaunt face was seized with determination. "We will proceed. Tell the others to be ready for their entrances." The two men hurried off, leaving Cindy alone.

It dumfounded her to think they would still try to play to that lot of ruffians. Her heart positively sank when she thought of Eric having to walk out on that stage again. Of course, he didn't have to, until the last act. Maybe by then he might pull himself together a little, she thought, if she could just talk to him.

Glancing around, she couldn't see him anywhere — not in the prompter's corner or working the curtain. Nor was he with Maud, who was tending Lorna. They had stretched her out on the couch over to one side. Helene sat weakly in a chair nearby, while Ralph tried to steady her with smelling salts. They didn't seem to need any help, and Cindy was pretty sure that Eric did.

Outside the men's dressing room, she called him softly, but there was no answer. And then it occurred to her where she would go if she were him. Setting the back door ajar, she peered out into the darkness. He was sitting there on the steps of the van in the moonlight. Didn't even move when she came over and touched his arm.

In a hopeless voice he asked, "Is — it — over?"

"No, they're going on. I think Brutus is crazy; he's out there now, doing his scene. So you'll have to, too, I guess, even if the people — Well, listen, you've got to forget them!" she implored. "Don't even pay any attention to their fool talk. Just hate them. It's the only way — hate them real hard, and then you won't care, it won't matter, they can't bother you."

As she talked Eric raised his head. "The audience? Hate — the audience?" The warmth seemed to be coming back into him fast. "Is that what you said — hate — ?" He began to laugh, ha-ha-ha, right out loud. Cindy thought he was going to have hysterics too, he laughed so convulsively. Anxiously she looked around for help, dashed back into the building.

But they were changing scenes there. Everything was a rush, setting up the graves for the churchyard. Ollie motioned her to help, and she had no chance to tell anybody that Eric was going all to pieces out in back. By the time the props were in place, she saw the boy come in and take up his position, ready to work the curtain ropes.

He was still red in the face, but he seemed somewhat steadier. He wouldn't look her way, though. And when she started toward him, Brutus got hold of her and guided her firmly out front again, where the crowd greeted her warmly.

"That's sure one useful little tyke," announced one man, "whatever she's up to."

When she reached the piano bench again there was no time to tell Durango what had happened. The curtain was going up and he was too busy with the accompaniment — watching the action on stage closely, suiting the soft melodies to the very movements of the actors. She'd never heard him play so skillfully.

Or seen Brutus put quite such emotion into his acting. Especially when he clapped a hand to his brow and said: *"I've borne an eternity of suffering . . ."*

He got the audience pretty well stirred up. And of course they whooped every time Ollie came on stage. He was at his funniest, strutting and bumbling around, pretending to be tipsy, falling over the scenery, trying to put his gloves on backwards. The miners guffawed and stamped their feet.

Somebody hollered to him, "You better git home to your missus." But by now the actors had got used to the outspoken remarks from the audience, and went straight on with their lines.

When Helene appeared again, however, at the first of the next act, she could hardly keep her face straight as she spoke her part, in an odd extravagant way. It was as if she were playing a farce and it wasn't a serious business, her poor old father going to jail. For the first time, the crowd fell silent. And somehow their sober watchfulness worried Cindy more than their earlier good spirits.

Finally the moment came for Eric's last appearance. Cindy listened for the cue with a sort of dread. And then, there he was, stepping out on stage, but speaking differently now, in a blunt, bold way. He never faltered once as the scene rose to the climax, where he shook his finger at the villain, Brutus, warning: "*If you do aught to injure my Mary, sink me if I don't pour such a* broadside *into your* buttock-shrouds, *it'll disable you for the rest of your life!*"

The crowd let out a roar of approval. The miners were cheering, calling out, "That's the way to tell him!" "Go to it, sailor!"

And one — the man who'd been doubtful in the beginning — looked straight at Cindy and nodded. "I'm glad!" he said loudly. "The boy turned out real good."

It seemed to Cindy like a miracle that they had not only got through the play, but the audience had gone away happy as if it had been a first-rate performance. The troupe knew better, though. They moved along in a hush as they went back to their rooms that night. Brutus was silent. Hard to tell what he might be thinking as he requested them to be present for a meeting next morning.

At ten o'clock sharp they were all gathered nervously in the largest room of their quarters. A sort of dining hall it was, furnished with a dozen chairs and a big rough-hewn table held together by great iron nails. A crude table, but Brutus stood at the head of it, regal as a king. Thumbing through his ledger he was tearing out the pages as he came to them.

"To Helene, the sum of seventy dollars, silver." He

pushed a canvas money sack across the table to her, crumpled the ledger sheet, and tossed it over his shoulder.

"No little fines deducted? How sweet of you, Brutus." She tried to speak lightly, but her voice was shaken.

"Not at all," he replied evenly. "The Green Room Rules apply only to professional actors. I was in error to invoke them against a company of amateurs."

"Now just a moment, sir! I resent that!" Ralph started up, but Brutus had found his page now and tore it out with some fervor.

"Resent away, all you like. I've resented your recent preoccupation with matters other than the art of the theater. So, with the payment of sixty dollars — there you are — I now return to you the absolute prerogative of pursuing a new career. I trust the panning of gold will be uplifting. Let's see now. Lorna — "

"Don't," she cried out, the tears standing in her violet eyes. "Don't tear mine out! Please, Brutus. I know I was the ruination of everything last night, but I feel much stronger today."

"Illness, my dear, is a misfortune for which I'd never blame you. It's another matter to work yourself into a state of palpitations over a reluctance to play the role you were assigned." He tore out her sheet, though more gently, and handed it to her with her earnings. "When I rescued you from an uncertain future in New York — a career of minor parts in minor plays — you seemed to welcome the chance to show your versatility. In fact, all of you professed to want to act, to reach audiences. I wasn't aware that there were limitations to your enthusiasm for the project."

The words fell upon them like a dread condemnation. Cindy clutched her little sack of money, twelve dollars and fifty cents, and she hadn't even dared look at it yet. This was too serious — happening just the way Durango had said it might, the troupe breaking up. Her security and all the rest — this was what he'd meant. Only where *was* he? Of all times to be late!

And now Brutus was paying Ollie and Maud. They seemed to accept his decision as inevitable, sitting there soberly. Only once Maud turned a dour look on the rest of the company. "And Ollie composed such puffs for the posters, about what a gem of a troupe we are!"

Ollie smiled dryly. "Should have read more properly, 'The Braithwaite Bunglers will blunder through a melodrama if the buffoons can bolster their bravery.'"

"And if the leading lady decides the audience is suitable," Brutus added.

Helene's chin came up sharply at that. "I could have had the audience at my feet if it weren't for that atrocious piano player. He stepped on my lines! I told him afterward in no uncertain terms that if he ever did such a thing again — " She broke off as they all looked at her, startled.

"You — did — what?" Brutus was finally shocked

out of his rigid composure. "You dared give the tip of your tongue to the one person who saved the troupe from complete disgrace last night? For your information, Miss, our musician was doing you a favor, to drown you out. You were insulting the audience with your obvious contempt, and too haughty to realize that they were growing aware of it. Durango saved us a dozen different ways last night, and now you have run him off! Well, it grows more evident than ever that it's high time to close the books on this company." He shut his ledger with a snap.

"Run him off?" Lorna echoed faintly.

"Durango?" Ollie looked shocked and Maud clicked her teeth.

"I didn't do any such thing," Helen began, "I only — "

"He's gone. He was up and away before we rose this morning," Brutus told them, suddenly weary. "And now I take leave of you, also. I must go to the theater and remove the poster advertising tonight's performance, thus disrespecting one of the proudest traditions of all — that 'the show will be presented as billed.' " Putting on his tall hat, he bowed to them with a mournful sort of elegance and went out.

"Oh, we are truly ruined," Lorna moaned, plunging her face in her hands.

The minute the door closed, a small pandemonium broke over the room. Cindy could hardly think through it; her own emotions were all scattered. *Du-*

rango gone? But he'd never leave on account of any-thing Helene could say. It must be because the man recognized him last night. So maybe he *was* an outlaw and she should be glad he was out of the way. But the thought of him leaving so suddenly — hurt. Confusing, because she knew she had no right to feel deserted, but she did. Cut loose from everything she had counted on — her job, the troupe, these people.

Ollie was holding up his hand for quiet. "Come now, we can't let this happen. We've got to stop sniping at each other and think." The rest of them hushed, looking to him anxiously. "We've got to get Brutus back. Or better, go to him with some proposal, some firm proof that we're not the duffers he takes us for. What we need is a mediator, and the boy may be the key to it." He turned to Eric who had sat, indrawn and brooding, during the whole affair. "How about it, lad? Will you serve as peacemaker?"

As he got to his feet Eric seemed lanky and young and tousled. Then he shoved the hair back off his fore-head; something tightened in his face, the square of his jaw. It was suddenly more noticeable — his resem-blance to Brutus.

"I'll be lucky if I can make my own peace with him," he said. "All he's done for us — don't you sup-pose it's taken more out of him than anyone, to drive us as he has?"

Ollie nodded vigorously. "That's the truth. That's what we must convince him, that we appreciate it. And you're the lad who can do it. He's told me that you were the real reason he formed this troupe. He wanted to teach you the craft of the stage from bottom to top."

Eric's eyes widened for a moment, then he shook his head. "That may have been part of it, but it's a lot more than that. He's always had a dream — of building a great traveling company, to bring the best of the theater to people who've never seen it. People in frontier towns, men like the ones last night — to — to scatter a little magic across their dusty lives. You should hear him talk of that some time!" He bit his lip angrily. "But you'd not understand it. You're all only concerned over your pay and your — your applause. You don't really give a snap about the people out front. And I forgot too, until — " he gave Cindy a swift look — "somebody reminded me. I just hope I can explain that to my father." He swung around and hurried out before they could say another word.

A new babble of protest broke out. Ollie threw up his hands in disgust. "Well, perhaps he was right. You're so busy defending yourselves, thinking of your little egos, then we should indeed disband. Fly to the four winds!"

But Cindy didn't wait to hear the rest. She had skirted the room and now she slipped out. The last words followed her, down the long flight of dark stairs, into the street where the world was going on about its business as if this were just another sunny day. Wagons bumping along the rutted road, men calling out to each other — she moved through the noonday bustle in a daze.

To have to start running again, being alone. And twelve dollars and fifty cents wasn't a whole lot of money to get from here back to — anywhere. This was what Durango tried to warn her about, all right. The troupe, going to fly to the four winds. And just when she'd got a small sense of belonging — now, to be a stranger to everybody on earth except her mother, wherever she might be. Her mother and — And nobody else.

But Cindy began to walk faster. Hurrying toward the livery stable. Durango might have rented a horse, which would mean he would probably bring it back. Outlaw or not, she knew where he stood on the subject of horse stealing.

When she burst in at the double door of the big barn the stableman looked up from his sweeping. A homely fellow with a thick, seamy face, so rough-looking she almost drew back from him. But then he began to smile shyly.

"You're the little gal from the play-actors. I seen you last night." And when she had put her question, his whole leathery countenance seemed to spring open in a wide grin. "The piano feller? Yep, he come in here early, wanted to rent a horse. But I wouldn't let him do it. No ma'am, I wouldn't. I *gave* him one. Told him to keep the critter as long as he wanted. Anybody that can bang out tunes like that! I never heard the like. Oh, he'll be back tonight, all right, he's got to play again. And I'm gonna be there, you bet." He fingered his stubble of beard. "May even get me a shave, by jing!"

As he went on sweeping, Cindy edged away toward the rear of the stable. It was odd — just the song he was whistling — it made her miss Durango acutely. She felt prickly; her heart was beginning to flutter and jump the way it did when she was about to bust off running. All that held her was the thread of a tune — the stableman began to sing under his breath.

". . . bet my money on the bobtail nag . . ."

But what she really heard was Durango's voice, talking along in short snatches: ". . . a shade young to be making your own decisions . . . better be thinking about that . . ." If she could ever be that cool about anything! Weakly she sank down onto the bench just outside the back door of the barn. Set herself to remember everything she could that he'd said to her that day.

Something about motives. "What makes Brutus tick?" And now she had the answer to that; Eric had told them. To build a great troupe, put on wonderful plays — nothing but the best. And it was true; nobody had worked harder than he did, trying to make them do better and better. So could he really stop now? What else would he turn to?

She sat stock-still as the discovery took hold on her: Brutus wasn't going to give it all up. He never meant to, and the others would realize it — Ollie already did.

They would go to him and convince him, and he'd take them back because that was what made them *all* tick. Cindy began to breathe a little steadier. They were probably at the theater now, making it up with him. They'd start rehearsing *Lost in London*, and pretty soon she'd go and make snow, because it was all she could do, too. It was going to be all right, except for one thing . . .

As the sun dropped lower toward the Divide, a hush lay over the stableyard. She tried to be patient, to keep that narrow bit of calmness and not question it. A good thing she hadn't started running again, plowing off blindly. Right now she sat, just listening.

The stableman had gone off to catch a nap — she could hear him snoring in the tack room. And beyond, from the street came the distant clop of hoofs as men rode past. Until at last one separated from the rest of the sounds out there and turned in at the stable.

Starting up softly she pressed her face to the crack in the rear wall, and a long shivering breath went out of her. Even in the dimness of the barn, there could be no mistaking the square shoulders, the slant of the flat-crowned hat.

Durango was talking to the horse under his breath. "Seems your master's pounding his ear. I guess it's up to me to pull your saddle."

And then someone else strode in at the front of the building. "Ah, my friend, I saw you ride in!" No mistaking Brutus' tones, warm with relief. "I feared we had lost you permanently, thanks to Helene's tart tongue. I must apologize — "

"Not at all. I've known so many prima donnas, they don't arouse me much," Durango said easily. "Except to produce a certain yen for a few hours' solitude. Besides, I knew you'd be coming to grips with your actors this morning, and since I'm not a permanent member of your group, I preferred not to be a factor in it. That's really why I absented myself today."

"You missed one of my best performances," Brutus told him wryly. "I disbanded the company — lock, stock and props. Heaven help me, it was a dastardly piece of deceit — me, threatening to take down the theater bills. Rather than do that, I swear I'd have put on a one-man act tonight, even if it meant doing all the Shakespearean soliloquies back to back."

Durango laughed outright. "I trust that won't be necessary."

"No, I think I managed to impress them finally with the seriousness of the situation. And with the help of Ollie they came to me with a good, sound proposition. They've bought into the enterprise. It gives us the working capital to go on, and as shareholders perhaps they'll feel a more personal responsibility. If not — well, I've told them that this is our ultimate and final test, and that was no bluff. I'll not go through this again. As it is, what with the hectic events of the day,

I've come up with one unsolved problem. In the confusion, somehow we seem to have mislaid Lucinda."

Durango stiffened. "What do you mean, sir — mislaid?"

"I mean that she's nowhere to be found. We've all been on search for her, but — Well, confound it, Durango, she can't have strayed far."

"That girl doesn't stray! She moves like lightning. I told you that in the beginning." His tone was so furious, Cindy was awed. Even Brutus seemed a little scorched by it.

"And I have done my best — "

"Your best? You've neglected her at a time when it must have seemed as if the world was coming to pieces around her. Sent her off headlong again. It's exactly what I didn't want to happen!"

"Well, she can't have gone very far. With her small fund of earnings —"

"*You paid her today?* Great balls of fire, man! With a little money in her pocket she could be on her way to Denver or Kansas or who-knows-where. Hurry — there's no time to be lost. We'll check the stage station first —"

"The others have gone to the theater to rehearse. She may have turned up there by now," Brutus began. But Durango was on his way out of the stable.

"I'll say this, if we don't find her within the hour, you may consider yourself minus a musician."

Stunned, Cindy stood motionless until she was sure

they were gone. Hardly able to take in the full import of it, or figure what it might come to. The one thing she knew for sure was that she'd better get over to the theater and join the rest of them. Right away.

15

THE WAY DURANGO had looked at her — it gave Cindy
mixed feelings of uncertainty and a sort of pride. She'd
really fooled him this time by not running away. But
she wasn't sure why it mattered so awfully much.
When he and Brutus arrived at the rehearsal and dis-
covered her, a swift expression of pleasure crossed his
face. It was as if he had regained some possession — so
keen a look that it stuck with her on into the late hours
as she tossed in bed.

She couldn't go to sleep because every time she
closed her eyes, an image of Durango would come
drifting along. Not really him, with his hat and
everything — just his *look*. Something that wasn't real,

but was there in the darkness just the same. It made her feel funny, and she kept glancing around. Not that the look frightened her; it made her feel oddly better that she wasn't there in the little room all by herself.

It seemed foolish now, in the sunny brilliance of a cool summer morning. Everybody was in good spirits. *Lost in London* had been a great success, and a bunch of the miners had even turned out early today to help the troupe pack the scenery and props. So now at ten o'clock they were all ready to go.

Durango, quiet and unreadable as ever, was on the driver's seat of the covered wagon with Eric beside him and the women were climbing in. As Cindy started over that way, though, Brutus crooked a finger at her.

"Ollie and Ralph will be riding with the girls today, to discuss some financial details," he said, "which gives me the welcome opportunity to have a little talk with you, my child." So there was nothing for Cindy to do but go ahead and let him boost her up onto the high seat of the van. She supposed she was going to catch it now, for being gone yesterday.

When she had finally hurried in on the middle of the rehearsal, the women fluttered around her for a minute, wondering where she'd been. But Cindy just told them she thought the show was called off, so she took a walk to get a breath of fresh air. And then when Durango and Brutus came, everybody made such a fuss over the piano player there'd been no time for questions.

Now, as Brutus swung up beside her, he looked full

155

of some intention. The covered wagon was already moving, with Helene poised in the back between the parted curtains, daintily waving good-by, which sent the crowd of men into a new spasm of hat flapping. They let out a cheer as Brutus picked up the reins and lifted his tall hat in a final salute. Then, with a mighty "Ha, there!" he started the horses. They threw their weight into the harness and the van began to roll.

Cindy was glad to see that the road veered away from the range of peaks to the west, heading out northward along the same high valley. It was easy going, and yet she sat there tensely, hanging onto the wagon seat with both hands.

"A beautiful day," he remarked after a while. "Hardly hot enough to bring the dew out upon your fair young brow. Are you disturbed, my dear?"

"Well, I know I missed part of the rehearsal yesterday." Cindy thought she might as well plunge in and get it over with. "I guess you're going to fine me or something?"

"Under the circumstances, let us say that was excusable. Furthermore, as a general factotum — "

"A what?"

"A performer of odd jobs — in that capacity you need instruction, rather than penalties. As a matter of fact, I had thought to speak to you about the character, the nature — the personality, even — of snow."

Cindy's thoughts scrambled away in a new direction. Snow — ?

"Imagine your emotions," he was going on, "if, some wintry night, the snow became unreasonable. Suppose you glanced toward the windows and found a veritable blizzard occurring at one and, at the other, only a flake or two falling. Wouldn't you be disturbed?"

That was because she had almost upset the whole box of cotton last night. Cindy knew right away what he meant. She had to smile, though, at him talking as if it were a real storm she'd made.

He nodded. "You feel it's a bit ludicrous, eh? Ah, but suppose you were one of the audience? Then it becomes more serious."

"It does? I mean — they didn't really think it was snowing."

"And there's where you are in error, child. They did — at least they should have, if they were truly wrapped up in the streets of London, the loves and deaths and problems of another time and place. All of us on stage were captured by it. We had all escaped this work-a-day world for one of imagination that's more real than reality. The men in the audience had been transported outside themselves — like gods, sitting back and witnessing the struggles of poor mortals. A peculiar magic that can only be achieved by creating a perfect illusion — such a fragile bubble, it can be shattered even by one wrong snowflake."

Brutus was speaking so earnestly, Cindy was impressed. "I'll try to do it better," she promised.

"We've all got to try harder. None of us has put

forth his utmost, with the possible exception of your friend, Durango." The careless way he left it hanging in the air, Cindy came alert. She thought he was waiting for her to say something about that.

Actually she wished she could. Since yesterday, she was more sure than ever that Brutus had made some sort of bargain with the piano player back in the beginning. And while it didn't bother her so much any more, she just wished she knew what it was. She thought she'd like to figure out what made Durango tick, that's all.

"An unusual man," Brutus was going on. "Particularly adept at keeping his own secrets. He doesn't seem willing to admit that with a little more information, I might be a better friend to him. And to you, of course. Ah yes," he smiled sagely, "I've suspected all along that there was more to your acquaintance with our musician than you revealed to us that first feverish night. You can confide in me, my dear. Whatever your relationship is to the young man, I promise to hold it in confidence."

Cindy could hardly believe it — Brutus was trying to pump *her*. Cautiously she said, "Didn't Durango tell you?"

"Only that he had an interest in your whereabouts. A difficult man to cross-examine. And at the time, I confess I was more interested in his talent than in his private affairs. He didn't strike me as having any evil designs upon you; he made no move to wrest you away from us. So I simply accepted it as a piece of rather odd luck that he agreed to come with the company temporarily. I say 'odd' because he would only accept the job on condition that we also provide employment for you. Surely you must have some clue as to what his concern is? I see you wonder why I'm revealing this? Ah yes, those watchful brown eyes of yours are quite expressive, my dear."

Quickly Cindy ducked her head and smoothed out a wrinkle in her skirt.

"It's quite all right, I'm willing to be frank. The fact is," Brutus admitted it almost regretfully, "the fellow has made himself quite vital to the company. So much so that I must be taking some account of the thought that he may leave us in the near future."

That had tripped Cindy, too. Ever since she'd overheard Durango mention it yesterday, she had tried to picture the moment when he'd tell them all good-by and walk off. And she'd know for sure that he was gone, that she'd never see him again . . .

"Come, come, child. You can trust me." Brutus leaned a little closer. "If there's anything amiss about the man, especially if he's in some personal trouble, we should know of it. Well, then, let's try another tack. You were afraid of him once — can you tell me why?"

Cindy shook her head. It seemed like a long while ago. But if he *was* an outlaw, she'd not have breathed it to Brutus for anything in the world — though why, she wasn't sure. Except that Durango, with his music and his horse-sense, was the only one of them all who had listened to her and really thought about her troubles. Yesterday he was the only one who had cared a hoot whether she was lost or not. But she could still feel Brutus waiting for an answer.

"I guess I was nervous because I didn't know why he was doing things for me," she said carefully. "I thought he was up to some trick."

"Perhaps he was — and still is. A strange trick on us all," the actor mused. "By being here, by throwing his considerable abilities into this enterprise of ours in which he claims to have no stake . . . What *is* his game?" His voice had quieted to a mutter as he seemed to study the wagon ahead. It was following a bend in the road, so the driver's seat was visible — Eric and Durango having some kind of lively discussion.

"There's something compelling about him." Brutus was talking more to himself than to her. "He can set a rhythm that will pull the whole company into step. I realized that in the midst of our trial the other night. But there are subtler influences that might come about as well. An unknown quantity — " Then he seemed to recollect that Cindy was listening.

"You see, my dear, we are really just beginning to breathe, as a troupe. And I, as impresario, am faced with the task of combining its elements into a single instrument of expression. You're a bit young to understand, but think of yourself as a collection of hands and shoulders and small, pretty feet, and leaping heart and racing mind — all to be controlled, if you are to be Lucinda. Now how could you manage it if you weren't sure, for instance, what one of your elbows might do at some given moment? Or whether your knees were stanch, eh?"

"I'll bet Durango never had shaky knees in his life!" She blundered out with it on impulse, and a smile touched the face of the man beside her.

"Quite likely true. But suppose he lends his steadiness to some of the others, then withdraws it. Where will *their* knees be?" And again he looked toward the wagon ahead, where Eric was nodding at something Durango had said.

"You mean — like Eric's knees?" Cindy asked blankly. "They got all right, didn't they? The other night, I mean, by the time the play was over."

"Exactly. And I keep wondering why. The boy had some experience that night which he won't talk about. I only know that someone worked a change in him."

"Oh. That was me," Cindy said. Then wished she hadn't, because Brutus was looking at her, his russet eyes suddenly probing.

"I noticed that you seemed intent upon distracting the boy — a very serious mistake unless you had some good reason."

"Well, I didn't want him to get so upset, so I told him something kind of silly, and he laughed so hard I guess he quit being nervous."

"Told him — what?"

"Well, it was about the audience. I know it was foolish, but anyhow I just said — well, you know — not to care what people out in front thought. I told him — Well, I just said, hate 'em all and then it doesn't matter if they like you or not." She had expected Brutus to laugh, at least a little. But he was starting to get tall and thorny.

"Child, child! What a disastrous thought!"

"Yes sir," she said meekly. "I know it. You can't hate everybody; there's a few good ones." And Cindy thought of the stableman with his face all coming apart with that smile.

"But to try not to care?" the actor groaned. "The point is to care greatly! Desperately!" For a minute he stared down at her, then the anger faded from his face and it took on a look of sadness.

"I'm sorry," she told him in a rush. "I won't ever pester Eric again, I promise."

"The real mistake was mine," he said slowly, as if groping for some answer. "Inexcusable of me to let even one small member of the whole go unattended. Yesterday, it seemed only a momentary carelessness. But now I see that I've neglected a whole vital principle: that we are bound together. All of us. Whether

162

for a few weeks or over the long haul, we must function as a company, in spirit and in fact. Though whether I can create a unity that will overcome the flaws of one part and the excessive brilliance of another — " Abruptly he slapped the reins across the horses' backs to make them step out. "In the next ten days, we shall see."

16

It discouraged Cindy, to think of ten long days when they wouldn't be coming into any towns. They were going to stop up here in the mountains and learn a new play.

Ollie had said all along they would need a spectacular one when they got to Denver. That was why he'd left this time open on their travel schedule. The plan had been to go on to the next place, Georgetown, and try to rent a barn where they could make scenery and rehearse. But yesterday, when Durango was riding around, he had come across some deserted buildings at an abandoned mine where they could stay free. And everybody was pleased — except Cindy.

She even wondered if he had some private reason for

wanting to hide them all away, back in a mountain canyon. It was only a few miles off the road, but as soon as they reached the timbered foothills, they were as isolated as if the rest of the world didn't exist.

The others thought it was great, though. As soon as the wagons had pulled up beside the two low log buildings, the men helped the women down and they all went poking around, exploring. There was a stream nearby, racing down fresh off the snowbanks.

Helene dipped a drink of water. "Pure nectar! It would sell for fifty cents a glass at Delmonico's."

And Ralph fingered the sand hungrily. The other men were carrying the trunks into one of the cabins. A bunkhouse, it must have been, for there were wooden frames built along the wall, just right to take a mattress. All it needed to make them comfortable was the feather ticking, which they usually slept on in the wagons. As Maud began to make beds, Lorna unpacked and Cindy swept the floor. Ollie and Eric finished the transformation of the place by hanging a curtain to divide the men's quarters from the ladies'. It was a heavy piece of stage drapery, painted to look like the wall of a handsome drawing room. Cindy thought it gave the place a ridiculous air of elegance.

Outside, too, there was an atmosphere of unnatural gentility. Under the pine trees the men had set out some living-room chairs which they arranged in a circle around a little gilded table. They set up a cookstove, too — another stage prop, but it really worked. Soon

Maud got a pot of coffee on bubbling, and the troupe was gathered about, in a happy chatter.

"All the comforts of civilization," Lorna said gaily as she handed out cups. "Now if we'd just set up a backdrop we'd be in the ballroom scene out of *London*."

Cindy puzzled over that as she sipped her coffee. Ever since her talk with Brutus, she'd been thinking how she was expected to believe in all their imaginary world. But she was afraid she was never going to feel as if she were really in London while the pine boughs shifted and murmured overhead, and the wind smelled of high-mountain flowers.

Helene took a deep breath of the cool air. "London be hanged. In this rustic arbor, I prefer to think of us as the unborn children of Paradise, preparing to descend upon the world, trailing clouds of glory."

And that just made Cindy more worried. Because if she was going to be part of this, as Brutus wanted, she was going to have to stop thinking about the plain truth — such as the fact that there was a wasp walking around on Ralph's collar — because it was going to break their bubble for them. In fact, she had just about decided she must have some flaw, all right, because she couldn't seem to get that wound up in it with the rest of them.

Ralph stood up now — the wasp flew off. Raising his cup, he said, "A toast, my friends! To our new play, whatever it may be."

As the others drank to that, Brutus went over to the

167

van and brought back a leather satchel. "Our first order of business — to choose just what we will lend our efforts to. And since I want to invoke the utmost dedication from all of you, I invite you to share in the decision." He dumped the contents of the bag onto the table — a jumble of thin paper booklets. Plays, dozens of them. Eagerly the actors drew their chairs up closer and began to rummage through the pile.

Ralph was quick to pick out one. "*All That Glitters Is Not Gold* — now there's a foolish title. Gold doesn't glitter, it gleams . . . Of course, the play itself is powerful."

The others had recognized favorites of their own. Maud was reading one, smiling as if she knew it well. And Lorna was leafing through another, wide-eyed.

"One wonders how they ever stage this," she murmured. "The heroine is stranded on an iceflow; it breaks up, right before the eyes of the audience, apparently."

Brutus nodded. "*Sea of Ice*. I saw it performed, most skillfully too. Great blocks of white canvas were slowly drawn away to the sides, revealing a very effective ocean of black silk surrounding the doomed woman on her little fragment. We must prepare ourselves to meet the challenge of the more difficult stage effects. These western audiences respond to action. They have a right to it, if that's what excites them. Let us not boggle at technical difficulties."

Ollie waved the play he was reading. "This sort of

thing should create a tremendous sensation. Criminal's out to do a fellow in and burns down the tenement where the man's sleeping. Ends with the whole stage a-fire."

Brutus considered it, but Helene was shaking her head fervently.

"Call me craven if you like, I detest stage fires. When I was appearing in *The Miller's Men* I lived in absolute terror of the moment each night when the powder magazine blew up."

They returned to the clutter of plays again, considering, discarding. Ralph tossed another one aside. "All about a couple of French kings. Can't imagine these mountain folk caring much for the trials of European royalty."

"Unless you could turn 'em into cattle barons," Ollie added. "Or better yet, railroad magnates. Now there's a subject dear to this whole territory — trains."

Brutus glanced up as if some idea had occurred to him, then began to hunt through the plays with a purpose. "Yes, here it is — the very ticket!"

They quieted respectfully as he went on thumbing through the booklet, nodding to himself. "By the eternal, I believe we could manage it. But let me describe it to you from the beginning — an exceptionally fine play thoughout. Good, sound dramatic elements, interesting roles for everyone, particularly Helene. It's about a beautiful young woman who was stolen from her crib in infancy by an evil old nurse — made to order for you, Maud. Her husband is an absolute wretch, named 'Byke,' whom I shall enjoy portraying. The two conspire to wring money from the girl's family."

"*Under the Gaslight!*" Ollie exclaimed gleefully.

"Yes, indeed. Made a great splash on Broadway."

"Good, you know it then." Brutus went on. "I see you as 'Snorkey,' the war veteran. He's a comic, one-armed fellow who helps the poor girl all through the play."

"I saw that, too!" Ralph interrupted. "There's a meaty role in it, the young chap who knows his love for the girl is hopeless but protects her gallantly nevertheless. Wonderful waterfront scene in which she's tossed into the bay and he leaps to the rescue."

"Wonderful!" Helene laughed aloud. "I accept the part. Watery graves for me — much safer than fires."

"No, no, you both survive." Brutus went on glancing through the pages swiftly. "This earlier action just leads up to the climax. The plotters have captured Snorkey and tied the poor devil to a railroad track — "

"Right there on the stage, center front!" Ollie was getting terrifically excited.

"The girl is locked in the station nearby, overcome with horror as the train approaches. She manages to chop her way out and drag Snorkey from the track just seconds before a passenger express blazes across the stage." Brutus closed the booklet with a snap. "Ladies and gentlemen, a locomotive — threatening death and

170

destruction, billowing smoke, churning wheels. Can we do it?"

"Bravo! I'm in favor!" Ralph broke into applause.

And the others were getting all worked up over it, too. Cindy thought it sounded impossible. She glanced at Durango, who sat over to one side, his chair tipped back against a tree. He was watching Eric. The boy had listened to the assignment of the roles with deepening disappointment.

His father noticed it, too. "There are a number of interesting lesser characters, enough to keep us all busy. Especially you, son. I see just at a glance a young gentleman in Act One, a lawyer in Act Two, the old signal man in Act Four — "

Eric nodded with a little disheartened smile, as if his thoughts were roaming off in some other direction.

"And finally we have a lively peddler boy, who contributes significantly to the amusement of the play, and even helps apprehend the villain in the final scene." Brutus seemed to hesitate, then went on with determination. "A role, I believe, which will be quite appropriate — for Lucinda."

Of course it was nice — the nicest thing Brutus could do for her and Cindy knew it. She'd never dreamed she would have a chance at a whole part of her own, with cues and entrances and exits. Yesterday she'd have been in a fling over it, but now she wasn't sure how to feel. What with all the mistakes she'd been making and not understanding the whole business, she had to consider the fact that if you don't do it right, you ruin it for everybody. It was a serious thought.

The women kept telling her how she was going to love it, and that she'd be a great hit — as if just hoping would make it so. But when she tried to ask them a little about how hard it was, they only told her not to worry. That's why Cindy had to get away for a while after supper and try to figure out for herself whether she could do it or not. Little William was one thing, but she even felt suddenly shy about that. Now that Brutus had told her how real it had to be, she wondered for the first time: What do you do, to die so perfectly the audience will really believe you *did?*

As she turned it over and over, she was wandering up the canyon toward the little grassy clearing beside the stream where the horses were staked out. Ever since the old roan went lame, she had gone and talked to him once in a while. He seemed like a lonesome sort of horse. Brutus had tried to trade him off in Fairplay, but nobody had any draft teams for sale. So they had kept him along, and now, there in the meadow in the last sundown light, she saw Durango hunkered down, working on him. At the swish of her skirts through the grass, he glanced up.

"I just came out to see how this old horse was feeling." Carelessly she flung an arm around the roan's neck. "Is his hoof better?"

"Improving. He'll pull his share of the load one of these days." Durango said it matter-of-factly. He didn't mean anything special, but it fit right in with her own misgivings.

"Brutus says we've all got to. He's going to make an instrument out of us."

"An instrument?" The piano player looked up quizzically. "You, too? So that's why he gave you a part in the play." He went on, then, swabbing tar on the horse's hoof. "I guess you must be fairly flattered, to join the ranks of the thespians. It's no child's play."

"I know. I know that." Cindy felt as if it was aging her, minute by minute. "You have to memorize all those lines. I never was any good at memorizing in school."

"Neither was I."

"You weren't? But you remember all that piano music."

"That's different," he said. "As a teacher of mine used to put it, some things you know 'by heart.'"

It seemed odd, to think of anyone teaching Durango to play the piano. And yet, of course, he had to begin sometime. Maybe when he was only twelve years old — Cindy couldn't imagine him being that young.

"A good actress," he went on, "must feel the same way about her favorite roles. You'll probably be right at home in the part of a lively paper boy."

Cindy almost thought he was teasing her, but she

173

could never tell with Durango. "Brutus wants me to go back to wearing my britches, so that I will. Feel like a boy, I mean."

He looked up — she thought some sort of shadow crossed his face, but he just said, "I suppose it makes sense. He's a perfectionist."

And though she'd never heard the word before, Cindy knew it fitted Brutus. "He says a play has to be so perfect, the audience really believes it — like magic — so they forget their own selves."

"That's where I'd debate him," Durango said remotely. "To me, the magic has always seemed to lie in making people more aware of 'their own selves.' But then I doubt if he'd welcome any argument. As he says, it's his troupe, and I expect he'll shape it to his own philosophy. Most of it . . ." He started up, wiping his hands on the turpentine rag and looking at her so intently, Cindy was afraid he'd start reading her thoughts.

She turned away and began to stroke the old roan's shaggy neck. And yet she needed to ask somebody about this new problem that had her so worried. "Suppose" — she was talking more or less into the horse's mane, as if it was just an offhand question — "suppose somebody can't be perfect, though. I mean what if somebody has a flaw in them?"

Durango didn't sound too concerned as he said, "Anybody's bound to have a fault or two."

"No, a *flaw*. That's worse. I know, because when

Mother tried to pawn her diamond ring, the man wouldn't give her much. He said it had a flaw in it. It's like a crack, I think." Anxiously she turned back to face him, but Durango stood looking out toward the stream.

"That's probably what my father was getting at," he mused, "when he told me I had an incurable weakness."

Cindy remembered the grim way he'd spoken of his father before. "So you went off and shot some wolves and — and he was wrong?"

"I went off and became a black sheep — and proved that he was a hundred per cent right."

Cindy thought he must be joking.

But Durango was completely serious, as he went on. "If you do have a flaw, you ought to find out about it at first hand. I don't mean you, of course, but anybody. Nobody should take somebody else's word for a thing like that. It's too important."

She nodded ruefully. "You need to know so you don't ruin things for people."

"No! No, that's not it." He looked around on the ground and picked up a chunk of stone. "This, for instance — see the thread of quartz running through it? That's a flaw in the rock. If I had a hammer, I could show you — it'll break right along that line."

Cindy stared down at the worthless fragment in his hand. She almost said *who cares?* Checked herself in time. "Why is it important, though?"

"If you were a prospector, you'd know. Because,

along that inner structure — that's where the gold will lie, if there is any. You never can tell." And with a sudden boyish gesture he spun the rock at the stream — it skipped across the water and was gone.

For some reason, Cindy began to smile. "If there really was some, we should have looked."

"Maybe. But then, I've always been more interested in other kinds of wealth. That's part of my incurable weakness." And Durango laughed with sudden humor — as if it were a good joke on somebody.

III

The Thespian

17

IF SHE could just ask her mother, Cindy thought . . . She picked up another saucer from the pan of hot water on the stove. Just the commonplace matter of drying the dishes had made her suddenly homesick. Not for Kansas, but for the old home so long ago where she had grown up, and where she and her mother had been close to each other.

After they'd had to leave there, they had always been on the move. Too many jobs and worries and counting their small hoard of money — no time to talk much about important things. Like people. And how do you know whether to like them or not? Jill Ferris always got a strange, knowing look as she'd say, "You should learn a few things from your mistakes." She could tell when a man was being deceitful. "I don't care for the way he avoids my eyes," she'd say. Or, "I worry that he smiles too much. No one can smile all the time and mean it."

Of course, you could never accuse Durango of either of those things. But suppose — Cindy was startled by the idea — suppose you did sort of start liking somebody for some *unknown* reason, and then they did turn out to be an outlaw. He'd even admitted he was a black sheep, which is probably how most outlaws begin . . .

"Angels and ministers of grace, child!" Maud's voice broke in on her sharply. "You've dried that saucer till the flowers on it are beginning to wilt. Here, let me have that." She took the dish towel from Cindy. "Run along in and help Helene with the beds. Maybe the two of you will rouse each other out of your whimsies."

It made Cindy smile a little. Helene was pretty much up in the clouds, all right, when it came to the housework. As she went into the bunkhouse, Cindy found the actress poised in the middle of the floor, holding the broom at arm's length. Regarding it mistily, she said: *"I forgive you. Yes, and I pity you — and so, good-by, forever."*

Briskly Cindy began to make the last of the beds. "Maud says hurry on and finish, so we can rehearse."

Helene laid the broom aside tenderly. "Always some mundane chore." And as she gave the comforter a shake, she added, "I thought the men were going to build the locomotive today."

"They've got it started. Ollie found a stovepipe in the other building, Eric's making a smokestack out of it. And Durango's figuring how to make the round part of the engine. He's seen more trains than anybody else here. I guess he's been around in a lot of places." Cindy thumped the pillows thoughtfully. "Where's Hoboken, anyhow?"

It was a chance question; she hardly expected Helene to look so startled. "Why — it's in New Jersey. A quaint old village on the shores of the Hudson. Ah, the beautiful Hudson, with its Palisades, its little ferries bobbing across — "

"Would there be a lot of prima donnas living around there?" Cindy wasn't sure what they were exactly, except that the big Barnum circus had one — she was a singer.

But Helene was being cagey now. "Is this some pretty little riddle that Durango has put you up to?"

"No. I just keep wondering where he came from," Cindy told her honestly.

"Straight from a hot room in Hades, where demons are turned into piano players, to fly forth and capture poor innocent souls with their fiendish music." Helene said it lightly, but there was a trace of spite just the same. She'd never forgiven him for playing too loud that night. "My advice to you, Little Cinders, is to stay away from him or you'll soon be in the clutch of his bewitched fingers. He'll lead you off like the Pied Piper, to some nether region where you'll have to dance and dance to his tunes forever." She spun around in the middle of the floor, waving her arms in such a wild imitation of madness, Cindy was glad it was only an act.

Jamming the comforter tight around the edges of the bed, she said, "No, I mean truly—do you reckon he's from the East?"

"I don't know and I don't care." Helene twitched her shoulders. "He's probably a wastrel and a bummer who's seen the inside of many a jailhouse. Let's not contemplate the man another minute. Come, brush my hair, there's a dear."

"Well, I should go and find Lorna," Cindy said. "My first scene is with her and she's going to practice it with me."

"Oh, we're an actress now. I forgot." Helene gave a slight laugh. "Well, go ahead, by all means." And she began to brush her own hair.

Skimming out of her dress, Cindy drew on the dungarees. They seemed rather tight. And the boy's shirt was straining at its buttons; she really had put on some weight these past few weeks. It made her feel strangely self-conscious to walk outside dressed like that. But Brutus had reminded her again at breakfast that he wanted her not just to act the part, but to *be* the newsboy, day and night, for they didn't have too much time to get the feel of their roles.

The bills in Georgetown called for them to present "A Premier Performance of a Startling Theatrical Piece never before Presented in These Parts" — and do it just a week from next Saturday night. So Cindy tried to concentrate, to put some boyish strut in her stride as she walked rapidly across toward the makeshift stage.

It was just a cleared spot in the woods, with drop curtains hung on three sides. Not even the proper scenery, either. They hadn't painted that yet, though Brutus was laying it out. He had strung up some canvas that they'd brought along, and was making bold outlines all over it in charcoal. As Cindy went past where he was working, he looked up and nodded.

"That's more like it. And I suggest you tie your hair up, as well. It destroys the illusion — it even gives you a womanish manner, to feel it dangling there."

Wonderingly, Cindy thought it was true. Just these last few weeks it had grown natural to have the long locks curling down the nape of her neck. They made it a pleasure to tilt her head or nod, just to feel them there as she walked. Now she made a coil and pinned it tight to her head, feeling strangely shorn.

And when she reached the stage, Lorna looked aghast. "My lands! I didn't recognize you, dear!"

Cindy stepped over the row of stones set out to imitate footlights. "Well, I've got to *be* this boy, and I almost forgot how."

Lorna nodded a little sadly. "But you're young —

you'll be more easily molded to it. The first thing to solve is your mode of walking, you know."

"I used to sort of bust along, people mistook me for a boy — at least some of them did." Cindy began to take big swinging steps around the stage.

"And move your arms, too," Lorna advised. "This little peddler is an alert sort of lad. Wide-awake people always 'toe out' and move their arms and hands about miscellaneously." She made some gestures to demonstrate her point. They seemed a little outlandish to Cindy.

"Maybe I could keep my hands in my pockets."

"No! That would indicate a very different sort of nature. Let me see if I recall what that signifies." Lorna tapped her brow. "Yes . . . the person who walks with hands in pockets and head slightly inclined is generally calculating."

Cindy paused to consider that. She'd seen Durango walk that way often enough. "Calculating about what?"

"Oh gracious, who knows? Maybe some real estate swindle, or perhaps a way to corner the stock market — plotting or scheming — anything."

"Are you sure?" Cindy demanded.

"Oh yes, it's a positive fact that you can tell a great deal about people by their modes of walking. For instance, fun-loving persons have a kind of jig movement — like this." She jounced a little as she took a few steps. "Unstable folks walk fast and slow by turns. One-idea persons are always very selfish and 'toe-in,' while cross people are apt to hit their knees together. And then you take the very observant ones — they walk casually; sometimes they stop and turn around, as their heads move alternately from side to side." She illustrated gracefully, cocking her head this way and that.

But now Cindy was thoroughly skeptical. Durango was the most observant man she'd ever met, and he wouldn't have walked that way for anything. Of course, he might be calculating, all right. He seemed to be up to something with Eric. She still wondered what they'd been saying on the trip up here the other day. It was even in the back of her mind to sort of hint around and find out, as she watched the boy coming across to join them now.

"Ready for the scene?" he asked Lorna, with his usual deference, but there was some air of restlessness about him that was only a recent thing.

"Yes — just let me glance through my lines again," she said, scanning the paper on which she had copied her role.

They'd all had to do it — spent most of yesterday writing down their own parts, taking turns using the booklet. Some of the longer scenes still weren't copied, but Brutus had made sure that Cindy had all hers down. She'd even managed to memorize this first one. It was a comical episode. Brutus explained that it was necessary to keep the audience from getting too gloomy. The rest of the play was pretty sad, all right. Cindy wasn't sure how she was going to manage it. Harder to be funny, she thought, than to have a serious part like Little William. But Lorna was supposed to be a clownish servant girl, so that ought to help.

She looked up now from her part. "All right. The scene begins where I'm polishing the stove — you're off in the wings." She motioned Cindy away to one side. "Now then, I have to drag you on-stage by the collar, and I'm not very good at dragging people. Don't put up much struggle, dear child."

"Wait," Eric said, "she's supposed to be carrying newspapers and trinkets for sale — pins, bottles of bootblack — " He was picking up pinecones and twigs, giving them to Cindy. She thought, with some relief, that would take care of her hands and she wouldn't have to move them about miscellaneously after all.

And then the scene was on. Lorna had grabbed her by the collar, hustling her into the middle of the stage: *"Here he is! He's the boy that sold me that stove polish what isn't stove polish!"*

And Cindy came back with her own line: *"What is it then — sa-a-ay?"*

Lorna gave her a slight shake: *"It's mud! It's mud at ten pence a bottle!"*

Cindy broke away from her and made a face, "*Ah, where could I get mud? Ain't the streets clean? Mud's dearer than stove polish now.*"

Trying to do it just as Brutus had explained it last night, she squabbled with Lorna until Eric came running on from the sidelines. It was amazing the way he could shrink down and look like another newsboy. "Peanuts," his name was, and he waved an invisible newspaper: "*Extra! Revolution in Mexico!*"

Cindy picked up her cue: "*Here, you just get out! This is my beat!*"

They began to argue and punch at each other, and Lorna chased them both off with an imaginary broom. That was all there was to that part of the scene. Cindy stood, breathing hard, a little amazed that she'd remembered every line.

"You weren't too bad," Eric told her, "but you need a basket to carry your wares. You can't hang onto them and fight too."

"And I need a broom!" Lorna said positively. "I just can't act like a servant girl without a broom. Where's ours?"

"Helene's making speeches to it over in the bunkhouse. Shall I go?" Cindy offered.

"No, you practice the scuffle with Eric. That's the hardest part of the scene." Lorna scurried off.

"And this time," he said, "hit harder. You're too kind about it, especially for somebody who — who hates people." He gave her a teasing look. It was the first mention he'd made about that awful night. Cindy grinned sheepishly.

"Even if that was a stupid thing to say, you were good, afterward. You really were." She grew more sober. "I thought Brutus would give you a bigger part in this new play."

"That's up to him," he said carelessly, only he wasn't feeling careless, she could tell. "Anyhow, these small roles are good practice. It's what you have to do, when you want to be an actor."

"Do you really? I mean, want to?"

His young face lost its perplexity for a minute and flared with one emotion. "So much — it's — that's all I've ever wanted in my life."

"Well, then I guess it's all right, you being bossed around by your father." Cindy nodded.

"I'm just lucky to have a great actor to teach me," he said with curious heat. "And he isn't bossing me. I could leave any time I want to. I could get small parts right now, back in New York, and play them any way I felt like. But what's so all-fired important about my opinion? Even if I do get an idea sometimes, how a thing ought to sound — But who am I? Why does Durango keep asking me what I think, confound him, I wish he'd mind his own business."

"Durango?" she echoed. "Has he been talking about gold and things again to you too?"

"No, this is different. He keeps agreeing with me! And it's beginning to get me all mixed up." Eric was getting madder, as if it had been right there at the front of his mind, waiting to go off like a firecracker. "Getting me to tell him how I'd do Ralph's role — I shouldn't even be thinking about it. I've got three of my own and yours to understudy."

"I didn't know that!"

"Yes, since you aren't permanent, I'm supposed to know yours. And Father wants me to learn Ollie's part — "

"But you'd like to do Ralph's?"

"Certainly. It's a great role, but it's not his type. He'll be too slick about it, and it needs to sound mixed up."

"You could do that all right," Cindy agreed.

"But it's not up to me to say what part I should play or understudy." Eric shoved the loose hair back off his forehead angrily. "And it's no business of Durango's either. Hang him! I wish he'd pick on somebody else. Stirring up a whole flock of notions I thought I'd got rid of a long time ago. Next thing, I'll start wanting to argue with people again. Well, he's not going to turn me all around! What does it matter to him, anyhow? And what do I care what some piano player says? I was doing fine before he got under my skin!"

Puzzled, Cindy said, "You were? You were doing fine when you were stuttering and all?" It was a natural remark; she hadn't meant anything by it, but it seemed to stun Eric.

He stared at her as if he were suddenly afraid. Then without another word he walked away — just strode off into the forest.

18

I<small>T WAS ENOUGH</small> to make Cindy keep an eye on Eric that week. And the curious part was, whenever he could, the boy seemed to be drawn back somewhere to the vicinity of Durango. Of course it might have been just chance; everybody was rushing around from one job to another. Cindy had never known people to work so hard. She had to hurry from early morning on, to keep up.

Brutus was everywhere. Directing the women about painting the scenery, putting the final touches on it himself. Cindy had helped do one whole "flat," the backdrop for the pier scene. While Lorna painted, Cindy made the stars. Cutting up slivers of silvery paper, she stuck them into the wet blue of the night sky, just as Brutus had shown her.

Then he'd be off to the other building, to check on

the locomotive, though that was mainly Durango's project. In fact, they hadn't even unloaded the piano since they'd arrived here. Brutus said it was to protect the instrument against sudden fits of weather, but Cindy wondered if there wasn't some other reason why he wanted the rehearsals to go forward without music for a while.

It certainly made everybody strive harder, Lorna said. Because they couldn't rely on the music for a mood, they had to bring it about with their own acting. In fact, being a thespian was just as hard as she'd figured, and more so. For some reason she couldn't seem to turn herself into a smarty little boy. A month ago she could have pretended it without half trying. Not to feel at home in the part, made her wonder if she was stupid or something.

Brutus had worked with her for hours. He'd told her every gesture to make and how to talk. She'd finally managed to make her voice crack beautifully when she said *"sa-a-a-ay!"* He'd shown her exactly how to hitch up her pants when she walked. And how to fix them too, by sewing patches onto the knees and seat and making little tatters here and there. Eric had given her a thread-bare shirt of his; she had to wear it tucked only half-way in, so part of the tail flapped. And the long sleeves kept getting in her way, which was supposed to be funny. Brutus even wanted her to carry around her props at all times. So the women had fixed her up a peddler's box, using Maud's mending basket and some thread and trinkets. Cindy felt a little silly lugging it with her everywhere — at first she did. Then she saw that the others were just as intent on their own roles.

It made her marvel, the way they could memorize whole pages and pages of dialogue so quickly. And how the parts took hold of them! Helene was so noble and full of suffering as she walked around the camp, she seemed in another world. And Maud kept sneering and cackling to herself as she went about her work. She hardly combed her hair any more. It straggled down fearsomely around her face, and she kept calling everybody "ducky" in the nastiest kind of way.

Ollie, too — he was in a perpetual twitch, jumping and squirming, as Snorkey had to do all through the play. He'd even taken to speaking like Snorkey in a fast, high, wistful kind of voice.

"Seems we're a bit early for the shootin' match," he remarked plaintively that next-to-last afternoon, as he and Cindy waited on stage for the others to gather for dress rehearsal. "I say, Miss, won't you help a poor single-winged soldier to button his tunic?"

"That I'll do, bub," Cindy grinned nervously. "But I'm no 'miss.' Why, I'll have yer know, I'm the peddler boy, I am." She was getting so that she could make up these little pretend-speeches fairly well. And he did need help with his coat; he had to keep one arm hidden inside it, so he was having trouble with the fastenings.

She went to do it for him.

"That's the ticket," he said approvingly. "A handy chap you're gettin' to be."

Dropping the false tone she asked him confidentially, "Do you really think I'm doing my part all right?"

"Why, fine! Fine! Doesn't Brutus say so?"

"He just keeps finding more ways I can improve. Every day he tells me something new to do, like turn my head — so. Or give a little kick with my heel. Only when I'm trying to remember all that, I forget my lines, or they sound awful."

"Then I'll drop you a bit of a hint." Ollie glanced around and lowered his voice. "Those instructions have probably all sunk in up here" — he tapped her forehead with his finger — "so don't fret over 'em too much. They'll stand by you when the curtain goes up. Once you get out in the lights, just enjoy your part. If you do, the rest of the house will too. No need to mention that to Brutus, either. He's a brainy fellow. He can keep track of all sorts of stage business, like a juggler with twenty balls going. But suppose we can't all juggle, eh? You take Eric, now — " He broke off. "No, we'd best not take Eric."

"He isn't getting the stutters again, is he?" Cindy thought the boy had seemed firmer than usual, the way he handled his small roles.

"Well, something's amiss or Brutus wouldn't be worried. Says he's going to spend all these last two days on the boy. Gave the lad strict orders, no outside discussions with anybody, especially piano players." Ollie's voice trailed off into thought and he glanced over at the locomotive.

It was really Durango's creation, but they'd all helped assemble it last night. And now it stood poised beside the stage. All painted glossy black, it looked like a real iron juggernaut until you got up close enough to see that the front parts were made of wood, and the round boiler, just canvas stretched over hoops of green willow, much the same way as the top of the covered wagon was made. There were driver-wheels only on the side that would be toward the audience — immense wooden disks with spokes painted on them, mounted one behind the other. They could spin like sixty-miles-an-hour, but the whole business actually rolled on two dollies, little skate-like devices that were mostly meant for handling heavy things like the piano.

The cab was the handsomest part, but it too was only half a box. On the audience side in gilt lettering were the words DENVER PACIFIC and up in the painted window was a painted engineer — a pretty good one, Cindy thought. Eric had worked on it hard late one night, after Brutus went to bed. Everybody said it was great, and Eric was fairly pleased.

After all the work he and Durango had done this week, Cindy couldn't see why they shouldn't be allowed to talk now, if what Ollie just told her was true. Aloud, she wondered, "Why is Brutus worried?"

"Hard to say," Ollie laughed strangely. "I guess

there's been a head of steam building, in that innocent-looking hull yonder. And of course we'd all like to see the boy keep from getting the pressure up again."

"But how?" Cindy insisted.

"Why, we shield the lad from disturbing influences," Ollie answered with a touch of skepticism.

"You mean Durango?"

"Hard to say. Don't know what to think about the piano player, I don't. Heard him having a go at Johann Sebastian Bach the other day. Don't suppose you've any idea where he came by music like that?"

Cindy didn't even know what it was. "Is it bad?"

"Could be pretty confusing around here — furiously independent stuff, Bach is."

"Listen," Cindy said, with all her pent-up puzzlement, "What do you reckon Durango does want anyhow? Why is he staying on here, making trains and doing work like that? Do you think maybe he could be — hiding? Maybe he's an outlaw?"

"Lor' love us, I hope not!" Ollie's little eyes popped wide. "Never thought of such a thing. We've all had our turn at guessing, but perhaps we'd better do some real investigating, eh? And I'm the man for it — 'I, Hawkshaw, the Detective' — one of my great roles." With a flourish he pretended to strip off a false beard. "We'll talk of this later. Right now, here comes the crowd — and who's that with 'em?"

A grotesque figure — an old man, to judge by his bent body and the wrinkled hands that gripped the long rifle. But his whole head was a mass of bandages and sticking plaster. There was only a mumble hole for his mouth and a single bright eye peered forth from all the swathing. As he scanned the woods around, he seemed to be only half listening to Brutus, who was ushering him along.

"We'd be pleased to have you watch our rehearsal, sir."

The old man looked at the stage vaguely. "Your what? What is this shebang, eh? How'd that railroad enjine git up here in the sticks? I don't believe it!"

"Come, sit down, my friend, and we'll show you a whole world of illusion." Brutus brought a chair but the old man shook his head.

"Ain't got time to watch no whatchamacallits, I'm bear-huntin'. Wait a minute, though, there's a feller I know!" He was staring at the far side of the stage, where Durango stood angled against a tree. Cindy wondered how he'd got there — just suddenly appeared. He hadn't been with the others as they came up. Now he regarded the old man tolerantly.

"I doubt if we've met, old-timer. Plenty of fellows in these hills look alike."

"They don't play pianner like you, sonny. Nor the harmonica like me, either. Don't you remember old Rocky Mountain Jim?"

At a stroke, Durango's lean face lightened and came unguarded. "Jim! Balls of fire, who could recognize you under all that finery!" He stepped forward to

shake the old man's hand. "What lit into you, a whole band of Apaches?"

"Nope, just one old witch of a she-bear. That's why I'm out here today. I've swore to devote the rest of m' days to the bear business. Before I'm through they'll wish they hadn't of tangled with me. Took most of my face and a whole patch of scalp I been savin' for some deservin' Injun. Oh, for bein' crool, there ain't nothin' like a bear." Jim's solitary eye fell on Ollie, who still had his arm buttoned inside his coat. "Looks like there's another poor feller that's run up against 'em. Where'd it happen, friend? If it's around these parts, I'll go after the animile — I'm out to get the whole bloomin' tribe of 'em."

"I'm a fraud, sir," Ollie told him with a smile. "No honorable wounds, just pretending. We're thespians."

"Hold on, now!" Jim took a firmer grip on his rifle. "Fraud and no honorable wounds don't sound so good. Sonny" — he eyed Durango dolefully — "I was afraid of this. Way you was carryin' on down Santa Fe, I figured you might end up with a bad crowd. Likely up to no good, runnin' around in their Sunday clothes out here in these woods." In a hoarse whisper, he added, "What's thespeens?"

"Actors, Jim," Durango told him. "They've hired me to make their music — it's an honest living. I've got a steady job."

It sounded as as if the old man hooted behind his bandages. "You — steady? What do they do, put hobbles on you of a night?" He looked around at the troupe more curiously. "Actors? The kind that does play-actin'?"

"We're about to proceed right now," Brutus repeated more insistently. "We'll put on a whole performance for your benefit if you'll have a chair, sir."

"I got a better idee." The old man wandered over onto the stage which was already set with furniture for the opening scene. "You folks come over to our camp tomorrow. We'll treat, by jing. Give you a turn-out and a big feed and even set up a kitty. You might take a likin' to gold dust, folks. The fellers over there would go plumb happy to see a real play."

Brutus smiled a little. "We'd be pleased to, sir, but I'm afraid there's no time left on our schedule. We must be in Georgetown by Friday to prepare for our performance there."

"That's all right; we're just a mile off the George-town road, wouldn't take you out of your way much." Jim bent and touched the couch in wonder. "That's purty, ain't it. Yes sir, going to be a real bang for them fellers. We'll even blow the whistle. Usually just blow 'er on the Fourth of July and Christmas, brings the boys out of the gullies."

"We had planned to spend tomorrow polishing some of the roles," Brutus began, looking around at the others. But Lorna was watching the old man tenderly, and even Helene seemed to have melted. Maud gave a nod, as if to register her vote. Brutus went on taking silent inventory of the others, ending with Eric.

Abruptly the boy spoke up. "I think we'll shape up better if we play to an audience, sir!" It seemed to break from him in a torrent, and then he blushed and shut his lips tight. Brutus lifted an eyebrow, but before he could comment, Jim was talking along again.

"Yep, we'll blow the whistle; she'll likely bring a hundred fellers down out of the hills. Purty fair whistle, brung out all the way from Pennsylvanie. That's why we call the diggin's 'Tin Hoot.' Leastways I think so. Mebbe it was on account of nobody gives a tin hoot about us old packrats up there."

With sudden decision Brutus laid a hand on the old man's shoulder. "My friend, you can go back and tell them we'll be there. Tell them that we'll try our humble best to present for them our premier performance of a new play, never before seen in these parts." And to the troupe he said, "Ladies and gentlemen, we have work to do, if we're to open tomorrow night — in Tin Hoot."

19

THE BEST — just the best they'd ever done! Even Cindy knew it, and the other players were so alive with the excitement, their scenes fairly sizzled.

Maybe it was because there had been no time to worry and build up that head of steam Ollie had mentioned. They'd barely reached the camp by sundown to find that there was no building large enough to hold the horde of men assembled. But the miners had worked all day to scrape a ledge along one side of a little gully and lay down boards to make a rough stage.

On the facing slope they had gathered in close-packed ranks, applauding every move as the troupe set up. Some had brought little packets of food; they sat gabbing and joking. Half a dozen of them hustled up on stage to help hang the curtain. Then Brutus sent them back out front to wait. He didn't want any of them around while the locomotive was being assembled behind scenes. When darkness thickened, they lit the footlights — their own lamps and lanterns of every description which they'd arrayed across the front of the stage.

So expectant, so ready to be delighted, they sparked the troupe to enthusiasm. It was clear from the minute the curtain went up that Brutus' instrument was in fine tune. There was a singing quality about the play as it raced along.

For just a minute before her first entrance, Cindy had stiffened. Her joints seemed to stick and, as Lorna hauled her out into the lights, her yelp, *"Let me go!"* came squeakier than usual. But the audience was tickled and their laughter braced her. They hooted louder at every line she spoke, as she swaggered about. When Eric came on as Peanuts she lit into him so vigorously that her basket of trinkets went flying all over the floor, and Lorna ran them off to noisy applause.

So far there had been only one near mishap. In the pier scene, Cindy had bent every effort to make the "water" billow properly. Crouched down out of sight behind the dock, she had rippled the sheet of green taffeta that covered the rest of the stage, making it work so rhythmically that it must have really looked like the ocean. Because when Brutus and Maud, the evil conspirators, tossed Helene over the back of the pier into the bay, a half-dozen men in the audience jumped up with drawn revolvers and Eric had to bring the curtain down in a hurry.

From the pile of feather bedding where she had landed, Helene flashed Cindy a grin that was positively mischievous. "Wouldn't it give Brutus a turn, to find himself lynched because of his troupe's sheer talent?"

But the real test was now to come. For the props were in place for the train-rescue scene. They'd laid out the tracks across the front of the stage and between them a strip of tin, so that the dollies would scoot smoothly across the loose board flooring.

"It's going to rumble superbly!" Brutus told them in a hushed tone, as they gathered around him for final instructions before the curtain went up. "The main element is split-second alertness. You all know your jobs — on your toes now! In your places!"

Cindy's post was beside the looming bulk of the locomotive. Eric was still on stage. He was the old signal man, puttering around the railroad station house, locking Helene inside "for her own safety" to wait for tomorrow's train. But as soon as his part was over, he hurried around to join Cindy at the engine.

"You'd better start the wheels spinning a good minute ahead of time," he whispered.

"Me? I don't know how!"

The boy looked puzzled. "Didn't Durango explain it? Just before rehearsal yesterday he started over to show you — Well, it's simple. There's the crank." He pointed out the handle on the far side of the boiler. By turning it, she could get the first big false wheel to revolve, and since it was attached to the second by a bar, just like the drivers on a real train, they both spun around together.

"Remember," Eric added, "there's only going to be a few seconds that the audience will see the engine. Father's going to bring the curtain down quickly, since we don't have the rest of the train to follow. So the wheels have to be already racing as it comes on."

Cindy nodded, but she was watching the stage. The play was getting to the crucial part. Ollie, as Snorkey, stood beside the track alone, scratching his head. He'd heard the villainous pair plotting new mischief and was trying to think how to stop them. And now Durango began to play a sinister theme, as Brutus came on, slick as oil, gliding softly across the stage at the rear.

The audience went into a frenzy, yelling to Ollie, "Watch out, man!" "He's got a rope — look behind you!"

But Ollie just stood there pondering until Brutus pounced, threw the rope around his victim. The struggle was on, but Ollie was easily captured and tied. Comically he quavered: *"Hello, what's up?"*

Brutus smiled dreadfully as he said: *"You'll se-e-e. I'm going to put you to bed."* And he hauled Ollie over to lay him across the rails.

Now Ollie began to look really scared: *"Byke! You don't mean to — Good Lord, you are a villain!"*

Brutus went right on gloating, though, rolling his words out in a frightening manner: *"You won't toss much. In less than ten minutes you'll be sound asleep. There, how do you like it, old friend? Dog me, will you, and play the eavesdropper? When you hear the thunder under your head and see the lights dancing in your eyes and feel the iron wheels a foot from your neck — remember Byke!"*

He let out a snarl of laughter that chilled even Cindy. As he sneaked off, the crowd was groaning, but when Helene appeared in the window of the stationhouse, they burst into a cheer. "Hurry up, ma'am, get 'im loose!"

She clasped her hands in an agony of horror: *"O Heavens! He will be murdered before my eyes!"*

And now the audience was on its feet, yelling, as Helene disappeared, came back briefly to the window flourishing an axe, then began to whale away at the door with it.

"The wheels!" Eric nudged Cindy. She seized the handle of the crank and began to turn furiously while he climbed up to drop a lighted match into the pan of oily rags hidden in the top of the smoke stack. They flared up, sending a billow of black smoke curling down and out over the stage.

"Hurry!" yelled the crowd frantically.

As Helene burst through the door, Eric gave a mighty heave and launched the engine on its way. With a horrendous rumble, it blazed out onto the stage, stack

206

spewing smoke, wheels racing, just as she pulled Ollie off the tracks. Swiftly the curtain came down.

And then Eric was hugging Cindy, Ollie squirming out of his ropes, doing a little jig. For all fury had broken loose out front. A roar rose that echoed far along the mountain slopes — it went on and on and on.

After it was all over Cindy felt a little caved-in. So wonderful. If only her mother had been there to see her — the thought seemed to hover like a mist, shutting her off from the elation of the others around her. Somewhere, a long way off, she heard Helene chattering as they all got dressed.

"You may give credit if you like to that fire-breathing monster, but I prefer to think they were entranced by me and my axe. Listen to them!"

Beyond the sheets that curtained off their dressing space, it sounded as if the entire audience had come backstage. Heavy voices, marveling over this and that in the play, telling what they'd have done to fix that villain right smart. "I'd like to have got my hands on that buzzard, mussin' up a lady that way, throwin' her in the ocean . . ."

Helene smiled at herself in the mirror. "Those gentlemen are certainly not waiting out there to fling themselves at the iron wheels of a stage prop." As she gave her hair a finishing touch, they heard Ollie calling.

"Hurry along, ladies. These boys are waiting to put on a celebration for us."

Cindy looked down at her dress — just the same old blue gingham she'd worn on the ride down. All at once she didn't feel too much like a party. As she followed the other women out, the men crowded around Helene — who wouldn't? Standing there crowned with that shimmering golden sweep of hair, she was gorgeous. Holding her arms out to them all.

"Wonderful, wonderful people!" she cried.

A few of the men glanced at Cindy curiously. It was plain that they didn't recognize her as one of the players; nobody would, of course. And then she saw Durango shouldering through the crowd. Dodging the bunch around Helene, he came over to Cindy.

"Does this party mean a lot to you?" he asked hurriedly in a low voice. "You've got a very special invitation to another get-together. Smaller, though — "

Shyly Cindy said, "I'd like that better." And somehow it hadn't even taken a second's thought to decide. She just hoped he meant they'd celebrate alone, the two of them, so she could put it right with him about yesterday.

Because it had come to her what must have happened. Eric said Durango had gone to look for her — probably just when she and Ollie were talking. He must have heard what she said and — whatever he thought, it was wrong! She hadn't been trying to point any suspicion at him. A sense of guilt came over her; she could hardly wait to try to explain.

As soon as they were free of the crowd he helped her

on with her coat, then took her arm to guide her along a dark path that led toward the ramshackle camp. They were really going somewhere — toward a cabin with a light in it.

"Jim didn't feel like a big nip-up," Durango explained. "He asked me to come to his shack and bring the little peddler along. He's gone ahead to put the coffee on. Said we'd know the place by the bearskin hanging on the porch." He helped her up the rickety steps and knocked on the door.

"Come on in. I'm pourin' the java!" The old man was setting out three mismatched cups. "How's this?" His one eye looked Cindy up and down. "That funny boy turns out to be a purty little female? I'll be dinged. Ye sure done some smart steppin' in that play, lass." Talking along, he ushered them in. "Set down, set down."

A small room it was, warm from the potbellied stove. Durango made himself comfortable on the sagging leather couch, leaving room for Cindy to sit beside him, while the old man lowered himself stiffly into the only other chair. As he spooned some of the coffee between his bandages, he said, "Well, well, we're some older than last time we brewed a pot together, eh, Paul?"

The piano player smiled. "Bound to be, Jim."

"If it wasn't for this dern-fool bear, took half my face off, can't tell what I'll look like when the medicine men get me all tinkered up — if it wasn't for that I'd say you've changed more than me. When I heard you work so careful with them tunes tonight, I knew it for sure. You used to play some wilder. I've heard you, times when I thought you was gonna shiver the walls out. Ever still cut loose like that?"

"Not quite." Durango looked into his cup thoughtfully. All at once he said, "What was I like in those days, Jim? I've been meaning to tell Cindy — she's got an interest in it. But somehow I've got a feeling that if I told her, I'd be too easy on myself. Would you say I was pretty much of an outlaw?"

Cindy almost choked on the hot coffee. Her cheeks were burning, but Durango wasn't watching her. And the old man's eye, deep in its bandages, seemed to focus on a long-ago time.

"Well, if you wasn't plumb outside the law, sonny, you was sure walkin' the fence. Racin' that horse of yours — Injun style, at that. Scrappin' and galavantin' and playin' hi-jinx. Remember the night in that Mexican den? Feller wanted you to sit in at poker, only you and me was busy makin' a little music. He got pestersome and you put a bullet right smack through the middle of his deck of cards. Whoosh! hearts and clubs all over the place. No harm in it, actual. But you was always ready to blow up — used to make me wonder if you wasn't gonna get yourself kilt. Never heard that you did, though."

"Almost." Durango laughed, a nice easy laugh. With his hat tipped back, and the lick of dark hair sprouting across his forehead, he looked younger than Cindy had dreamed. "I made a slight mistake. Took on three men in a fight — which was all right with me, but they happened to have three friends. A few hours later a fellow picked me up out of the street — more busted strings and loose keys than you could count. He helped me get back in tune."

Jim was interested. "Anybody I know?"

"Ever hear of Doc Durango?"

The old man slapped his knee. "By jing, I thought I heard something familiar in your playin' tonight. So Doc taught you some of his own tricks. No man ever handled them ivories better than him — only playin' I ever heard that could beat yours. So he's in Santa Fe now?"

"Not any more." Something tightened again in Durango's face. "He was ill when he took me in. But we got to be friends at the last, close enough so that he turned over a few valuables to me. Among them, his name. I've been somewhat more careful of it than I was of my own."

The old man considered that soberly. "Well, we all got to cash in some time. Which gives me an ideer. Wait here a minute, I'll be right back."

When he had hobbled out, the silence closed in on the room. Cindy felt somehow burdened by it, and by the far-off tone of what she'd just heard. "I'm sorry," she burst out at last. "Blabbing all that to Ollie — "

Durango waved his cup as if to brush the thought aside. "In a little while it won't matter any more what the troupe thinks of me. But you — ?" He looked down at her briefly, puzzled. "Ollie couldn't pry any information out of me in a hundred years, but you could have found out, just by asking."

"I — could?" she whispered.

And then old Jim came stumping back. In his hand was a harmonica, its gloss dulled by long years of hard use. "She ain't no good to me any more, that bear done ruint my pucker. But you used to be pretty fair on it, Paul. Go ahead. Try her out." He settled himself back in his chair. "Give us a little Shenandoah. Always reminds me of home."

Durango put the instrument to his lips, uncertainly at first, but soon drawing a powerful plaintive melody from it.

At the first notes, Cindy caught her breath hard. It was the same tune her mother used to hum sometimes, those last days in Kansas. The room blurred before her eyes and she clenched them shut tight. Wondering when . . . or where . . . or how there was ever again going to be a home for her.

20

A PANG OF REGRET pricked Cindy, now and then, as they made the slow descent down a long winding pass out of the high country. She kept thinking of those miners, even felt a kind of fellowship for the lot of them. Separated from their long-ago homes, their families, they lived a remote life with little pleasure in it, and she knew how that could be . . . Somehow it had all come over her, night before last in Jim's old shack. She knew more keenly than ever why Brutus had felt so shocked, that time she'd talked about hating the audience.

Tin Hoot had touched the rest of the troupe, too. For the miners had rewarded the company with more than thanks and gold dust. They had stripped their town of its one treasure. At the party that night, they had presented Helene with their whistle. A great ugly wonderful steam whistle that was exactly what the company needed. For, as one of the miners had said, "The only trouble with that en-jine of yours, it didn't have no toot."

So now they would have the real fearsome wail of a train whistle from offstage to herald the onrush of the locomotive. Helene had cried when they gave it to her, for the men had also decided on the spot to rename their town — Heleneville.

And Lorna was still daydreaming over her proposal. One tough old prospector had asked her to marry him. "I think he liked the way I polished that stove." She was talking about it now, in the rear of the covered wagon, with the other women and Ralph.

Cindy had got restless back there and ducked out to sit on the driver's seat with Ollie. For her thoughts were ranging ahead as they approached the lower valleys where the big camps were.

"You said there were lots of towns around here, didn't you?" she asked as they moved slowly down the long grade.

"Hundreds!" Ollie was in great spirits today. "These gulches are habitated with hovels, homesteads, harems, holes, hotels, hamlets and health resorts. The whole district's one big anthill."

Of course she knew it was expecting too much — that she might find her mother in the first place they came to. Cindy tried to keep her hopes from racing away downhill too fast, just as Ollie was holding the horses in tight rein.

The old roan was back in harness again today, to free Ralph's mare for riding purposes. But curiously enough, when Brutus decided to send someone ahead, he had chosen Durango to go. It had irritated Ralph, and even Ollie looked mystified, because it was usually his job to precede the troupe. Especially when they needed to get some supes lined up. Until now they'd had to leave out several scenes in the play for lack of enough people to take the small roles.

"I just hope the piano player can put his finger on the right folks to populate the play for us," Ollie remarked. "And by the way, I've got some clues for you on that fellow."

Cindy wriggled inwardly. She didn't want to listen, but she didn't know how to get Ollie to stop, now that he was launched on it.

"At the party the other night, people kept asking for him. I ran across a couple of fellows who knew him, even. He must have cut a bit of a figure around Santa Fe a few years ago. But that wasn't the part that intrigued me. No, it was his name — Paul Dexter, it is. Whole tribe of musical Dexters back East, which set me to thinking. The father was a master violinist; a few years ago I heard him in one of his concerts. A thin knife of a man, draws the longest bow since Paganini, according to the critics."

"Was he sort of mean-looking?" Cindy asked, thinking of the wolves.

"Severe — oh quite. And the talk was that he made his sons step lively to whatever tune he chose to fiddle for them. Six boys, he had. And then all at once there were five. The youngest kicked over the traces a few nights before he was to play his first concert. Reason I remember, it was a bit of a scandal around Delmonico's where we actors and musicians used to get together. That was in my heydays . . ." Ollie broke off, following some train of memory.

But Cindy was off on a whole new thought. For in the quiet they could hear Brutus expounding on something. A short way behind, he and Eric were driving the van. And now the deep tones of the father's voice rang out resoundingly, echoing along the narrow pass.

"At any rate," Ollie went on quickly, "the lad bolted — nobody knew where. Good deal of speculation that he went wrong. But then that's no affair of ours, eh? Doubt if we should even mention this to — anybody." Chirping to the horses, he sent them at a faster clip for the ground was leveling off. Through the trees ahead they could see the rooftops of a prosperous-looking little community. Over his shoulder Ollie called to the others.

"By George, it's Georgetown!"

That brought them crowding up to the front curtain. "Civilization again!" Helene waved her manicure scissors in salute. "It will jolly well have to exert itself to match the memory of Tin Hoot!"

Ralph was scanning the street ahead. "Do you see my mare anywhere?"

Cindy was watching for it too. But even more wishfully she kept searching the faces along the main street where people were pausing to look at the two wagons. Nobody she recognized, but her hopes picked up a little, for these were respectable folks, nicely dressed women, business men. The kind of place her mother might choose to live, it was a neater town than they had seen on the whole trip, with quite a few new buildings.

"Why it's positively first-rate." Maud put her stamp of approval on it.

"Wait till you see our theater," Ollie told them. "Fellow named McClellan must have dug more silver one day than he knew what to do with. Put up a hall worthy of royalty. Ah, here's the street. That's our hotel, there on the corner — The Silver Queen, brand new this year. And there you are, McClellan Hall."

"There's my horse, too, thank heaven," Ralph announced.

But the rest of them were staring at the building. A magnificent imposing edifice, as gracious as any big city could have boasted. Above its double doors in the finest lettering were the words: OPERA HOUSE.

As they pulled up at the stage door, they drew a cheer from the small crowd of men and boys waiting there.

"It's them!"

"Howdy, there. We're aimin' to hire on, like your fellow said."

Cindy was already clambering down off the wagon. Even though there was no reason to suppose it, she kept thinking that Durango *might* have talked to someone who *could* have heard about the dance hall girls.

As she ventured into the building, away from the commotion, a muffled richness seemed to close around her — of carpeting and soft hangings, and quiet music. From somewhere out in front came the sound of a piano. It led her through the handsome draperies, out onto the stage, and she saw Durango sitting below, playing.

He was so absorbed he didn't hear her at first. When she came down the steps to stand beside him, he looked up — somehow he just naturally included her in the music without stopping.

"A superb piano," he said, as if they'd been here to-gether all along. "The best I've played on in years." And his hands made a quiet, intricate progress up and down the keyboard, even as Brutus came striding in to stand at the center of the stage, surveying the theater with satisfaction.

"Exceptional, eh?" he said to Durango. And it was. With oil paintings on the walls to either side of the stage, and gilded moldings everywhere. "Well, sir," he went on, "I suppose you won't be needing our old box while we're here — easy to see you feel at home with this one. Though, to tell you the truth, I had rather you'd been out rounding up someone to take the part of the Judge in Act Two."

Durango went on playing without a pause. "The mayor of the town will be proud to do it. He'll be over to see you this evening."

Brutus looked slightly astounded. "I'd hardly have expected that. What did you offer him, sir?"

"The honor of it, of course."

Brutus smiled, in spite of himself. "You're a cool one, I must say. What the devil are you playing there, man?"

"It's a Bach fugue," Durango said, and Cindy could have sworn he slipped her a slight wink.

"Well, well," the actor said acidly, "you've got unsuspected talents. Too bad our audiences are a trifle too rustic to appreciate it."

"Can't tell," Durango said straight-faced. "I might use this as an interlude one of these evenings."

"About that" — Brutus frowned judiciously — "I feel I've been rather delinquent in not working with you more closely on the programming of the accompaniments. I'll try to remedy the situation from now on."

Durango regarded him agreeably. "Up to you. But it's only fair to mention that a third hand on the keyboard has always seemed to hamper my freedom. When it comes to being effective, that can be a great factor — freedom. Or don't you agree?"

Brutus seemed to read some extra meaning into that.

His gaunt face grew masklike and he spoke carefully, as if he were working out some part in a play. "A slight amount of discipline should be no hindrance to anyone who can master something as difficult as Bach."

"Discipline!" Durango seemed to seize on the word with enthusiasm. "Now there's an exciting business, if it's self-discovered. That's why I couldn't even handle this fugue correctly until I was free to experiment on it — and on anything else I might play, even if it's a tune about a bobtail nag. A strange compulsion, Brutus — to be your own man. A matter of decision, and to some people that's the whole love of life. Something you must understand, sir."

"A complex matter," the actor retorted curtly. "Too many qualifying factors in it to discuss here and now. May I remind you that there's a locomotive to be set up, the scenery unloaded. And Lucinda, I believe the ladies are looking for you to help unpack the props."

When he had walked off again between the curtains, Durango sat for a minute, his hands quiet. He seemed to be in the grip of some tough problem, to judge by the way his jaw was knotted tight. At last, glancing at Cindy, he said, "Steady does it."

And she knew he wasn't talking to her as much as to himself.

Something going on . . . the others seemed to sense it too. There was the sound of nerves in the way Helene raved over the pretty little dressing room that was to be all hers.

"Lovely, lovely!" She must have said it half a dozen times.

Ralph, on the other hand, was unusually snappish. "I cannot see why I must be quite so continually thwarted. I would rather like to take a ride on my horse. I've hardly had a chance, you know."

Brutus cut him off short. "It's somewhat more important right now that you help Durango assemble the locomotive. Eric is going to be busy with me all afternoon, reading parts with the supes."

"But couldn't we just go to the hotel for a little while, Brutus?" Lorna pleaded. "I'd like to freshen up."

"Very well. Be back here by four, please."

As they went out onto the street together, Helene waved her handkerchief as if to clear the air around her head. "What a mood he's in. I feel as if I'd been walking the rim of a seething volcano."

And Maud nodded. "I don't like it. Been building up all day — I could tell, watching him as we came down the pass. Couldn't hear what-all he was saying to the boy, but I haven't seen him so worked up since the time he played *King Lear*."

Cindy wasn't following the talk, though. She was thinking — four o'clock — almost an hour to look around. And maybe her only chance until tomorrow morning.

As they started up the hotel steps, she whispered to Lorna, "I'm just going for a short walk." And before there was time for any discussion she was hurrying on down the street. She thought there must be somebody who could direct her to a dance hall, if there was one.

Halfway along the next block she saw a likely sign — "The Pink Petticoat" — all decorated with lacey ruffles and curlicues. In the doorway a man lounged. He barred Cindy's way as she started in.

"No youngsters allowed, Miss."

"Is this a dance hall?" she asked, her pulse beginning to skip faster.

"We've got a few girls. You're a mite small to be thinkin' of hirin' on," he drawled.

"No! I'm looking for somebody. Jill Ferris — "

But he only shook his head. "Nobody by that name, not in this gulch. I know 'em all."

The flicker of hope died, but Cindy thanked him and walked on. She hadn't expected it to be easy. As she reached the corner she hesitated, wondering which way to turn, when she saw a woman sauntering toward her. Something familiar about the flirt of skirts and indolent air.

"Flossie!" she gasped. Then ran forward, shouting it — "*Flossie!*" One of the girls who had lived in the rooming house back in Kansas.

She stared at Cindy and a broad smile broke over her face. "Holy mackerel! It's Jill's girl. And all prettied up — I scarce knew you. What's happened to the tomboy?" She reached out and gave Cindy's chin a playful tweak. "You been minding your mother at last, letting her turn you into a young lady."

"*Mother?* I don't even know where she is!" Cindy's heart just about collapsed. "I thought she'd be with you and the others."

Flossie looked baffled. "Why the last we seen her, she was flying through that railroad station in Denver. The way she jumped off that train! Of course, she'd just spent the whole night blaming herself and us and everybody on earth for the fix you was in, back in Kansas. Wouldn't surprise me if she'd started walking back that way on foot. But if you're not with her, how'd you get up here in the hills?"

"It's — complicated." Cindy brushed the question aside. "Listen, where are the other girls? Or the manager — he might know."

"They're over in Black Hawk, honey. But I just come from there, and I can tell you, they haven't heard a word from her, either. I'm awful sorry . . ."

21

Cindy couldn't remember how she got back to the theater, or whom she told of her terrible news. She was aware of Lorna clasping her tight. Telling her never mind, the strength of a mother's love was like a magnet that would draw them together sooner or later. And Helene tried to picture how some day she would have her name on the bills — "Mlle. Lucinda Ferris" — and her mother would be bound to hear of it. The one thing that did strike through the blue haze of confusion was the way Durango looked at her. Cindy could almost hear him saying, "Steady does it."

But there was no chance to talk to him alone. Brutus was hurrying them into the rehearsal. Cindy moved through it, doing her part somehow, but mainly trying to think: what next? And the answer to that was coming clearer all the time. Go back to Kansas, the only place her mother would know to search for her. Might even be back there by now, or at least she could have written the sheriff.

The thought of giving herself up to the sheriff made Cindy's stomach crawl. And the awful question of lawyers and courts — yet she told herself grimly that it was the only way she could ever get in touch again with her mother. The thought took such a hold on her, she kept missing her cues and even forgot her lines in the last act. As soon as the rehearsal was over, Brutus paused beside her.

"A word with you, child. Come into my office, if you will." He led the way into the little room and sat down at the desk, while she perched on the chair opposite. He studied her a minute with a certain sympathy, and his voice was lenient as he said, "In Article Five of the Green Room Rules, it is set forth that a performer absenting himself from rehearsal shall forfeit four dollars. Would you say, my dear, that you were entirely with us this evening?"

"I guess not." Cindy tried to smile, because he was joking in his own way.

"I only mention it to pay you a compliment, in that I consider you a professional now. That's why I'm sure you can exert a little more concentration in the dress rehearsal tomorrow, and particularly in the performance itself. The most distinguished citizens of the locality will be attending."

"Maybe I'd better just quit now, so I won't ruin things," Cindy told him miserably. "Eric could play my part. I've got to leave, anyhow. As soon as I think how to do it, I've got to go and look for my mother."

"On the small sum you've earned? It won't take you far, my dear, and you're young. Too tender in years to be at large in a difficult world. No, you must stay with the troupe — it's your only security. And I believe I can offer you a most promising future, not just in the romantic roles, but the highest peaks of dramatic art — tragedy and comedy. The elements of both are already mingled in your young soul, just waiting for someone to mold them." He leaned toward her, the reddish eyes burning as if he saw some vision. "I shall shape you into a fine actress."

The intensity of the words frightened Cindy, the way he scanned her face as if already seeing it in some new shape. "No!" she burst out in spite of herself. "I don't want to do that. I just want to find my mother — she likes me the way I am, and so does Durango." She stopped short, wondering why she had automatically coupled him into her thoughts.

She could see that Brutus was considering that too. "The man seems to have made his opinion felt in more ways than one around here. How is it that you've rallied to him, after your one-time fears? I'd be curious to know."

"I guess it's because he helps me figure things," she said. And was surprised, since she hadn't really thought about it. "He doesn't tell me what to do — he never did call me 'child.'" The darker Brutus' expression grew, the more she felt defiant. "I bet he'll help me find my mother, too, if I ask him."

"He provokes a curious rebellion in young people — a dangerous ability," Brutus reflected. He was sitting upright as a stone statue at the desk now. "But as I see you rise to his defense, I must concede him one point. That you are not a child any more. All the greater need to begin at once the tempering processes that will turn you into metal which can strike fire from an audience! Tomorrow, we shall begin. To keep busy, my dear, that's the way to overcome our sorrows. And when doubts try to seize upon you, just remember that the tricks of Fate are ours to learn from. This may be the beginning of a great young career."

"But I can't *have* a career, I've got to go and — " Cindy fell silent, for Brutus just wasn't listening. In the excitement that seemed to burn inside him, he had forgotten that she had to decide for herself.

"Some day you'll thank me, Lucinda," he was going on warmly as he stood up. "But one word of advice, for your own good. Stay clear of our musician. He'll only roil the waters for you, and they're already turbulent enough."

And that was the truth, in a way. When she stood alone outside the office, Cindy felt as if a whole flood was tearing at her inside. An actress? A really great one — better than Helene, maybe? The thought swirled in her head as she walked through the wings and across the darkened stage with its shadowy scenery. But she knew she'd never be able to give herself over to this make-believe world. The hard truth would keep getting in the way. The real things — like Durango — maybe waiting for her right now.

Brushing past the big curtain she hurried out into the front part of the theater. In the semi-gloom it seemed huge, empty except for the man who sat at the piano. The lid to the keyboard was closed; he was leaning forward with his elbows on it, deep in some thought. When he saw her he stood up and held out a hand, to help her over the footlights.

As she jumped down beside him she said gratefully, "I'm glad you stayed. Brutus kept talking and talking."

Durango made a short sound that could have been amusement or irritation. As they sat down on the bench together he seemed even deeper than ever in that current of thought which had absorbed him. Sitting there with his hands on his knees — it struck her as odd, they were usually roaming the keys. Beneath the rolled-up sleeves of his shirt the strong sinews of his arms looked tense.

She wondered if it could be her own trouble that was making him sit so still. Cautiously she said, "I know you told me once you weren't going to worry about me any more. But now I — I kind of thought maybe you could tell me what to do when I get to Denver. Which is where I'm going to start," she went on faster, "but I don't think Mother's there. Flossie said she might have gone back to Kansas, so I suppose that's where I've got to go, even if they put me in jail."

"It won't come to that, I promise you," he said. But even though he'd heard everything she said, Cindy knew his mind was on something else. It made a little eddy of disappointment in her.

"What I thought was," she went on more slowly, "maybe you could tell me where to stay in Denver. I've got twenty-two dollars."

He roused at that, almost angrily. "Brutus hasn't exactly made you financially independent, has he?"

"He wants to make me a great actress," she said. "He wants to tinker me up, I think. With a temper and all, so I can set fire to people like Helene does."

Durango was startled out of his musing. "And yet you're ready to go back and face the sheriff instead?"

"Don't you think I *should?*"

"I think you could — that's the point." He spoke with a dry admiration. "Your flaws, as Brutus calls them, would look well on certain other people."

Which was all right, she was glad he thought so. "But what should I do?"

"I told you once — that's a question I can't answer. I may be able to suggest a couple of choices, but you're

229

going to have to decide. I only hope you'll wait until after the show tomorrow night. As a favor to me, if you will."

"The show? What's that got to do with it?"

"Everything. Everything depends on it going well."

"Finding my mother, too?" But he just wasn't thinking about that. He was all tied up about something else, probably Brutus. Everybody in the troupe was feeling the rub of friction between them now. Impatiently Cindy said, "I guess I've just got to go on to Denver without any advice and if I get kidnaped by a Taos trader —"

"— you'll regret it," Durango finished with a fleeting smile. "I'm not putting you off, Cindy. I *can't* help you until after tomorrow night. And when it's over, you may not even want any advice from me." Intently he looked at her. "Will you wait that long? Please — stay and go through with the show, play it as you never have before. There may be a whole future at stake."

It meant he was up to something, just as she'd already begun to expect. "Whose future — Brutus's? *Or Eric's!*"

As Durango turned back to lean on the piano again, he laughed with that touch of derision. "No," he said. "Mine."

22

WHEN SOMEBODY like Durango asks you a favor,
Cindy thought, it's no light whim. With a touch of
pride, she set herself to concentrate that next morning.
Brutus and Eric were rehearsing the supes, and she'd
offered to help — mostly to show Durango she was
going to do her best. He was there, too, playing tireless
background music, but as withdrawn as ever. Cindy
couldn't even imagine what he might be up to, until it
came time for dress rehearsal that afternoon and somebody remarked that Ralph was late.

Maud offered to read his lines so they could go on
with the rehearsal. Brutus agreed, but he was furious.
And Cindy began to have an inkling. She kept watching
Eric. As the time drew on, later and later, he was visi-

bly bracing himself. His readable young face took on a growing excitement that was part wish, part fear. Not that he was in cahoots with Durango — didn't even look toward the piano player once. But Cindy had an idea what the point of all this was.

By mid-afternoon Brutus was looking at his watch every two minutes. He had sent someone to search for Ralph, and when the man came back, unsuccessful, it put them all into a buzz of nerves. As soon as the last scene was over, Brutus called the troupe around him; his irritation had settled into a serious anxiety.

"This has reached the point of crisis, ladies and gentlemen. The stableman says that Ralph left early this morning in company with an Indian. I begin to fear foul play."

"An Indian?" Durango paused in the act of lighting a cheroot. "That may explain everything, if it's the same fellow who pestered me yesterday when I rode in. Wanted to show me where to look for nuggets. The usual story — he knows a secret canyon north of here which he'll reveal for a price. Those fellows will do anything for money. I told Ralph to steer clear of him."

Brutus was glaring. "You showed poor judgment even to mention the subject of nuggets to Ralph. But no matter what caused his temporary defection, he should have come to his senses by now."

"I hope they're fairly keen," Durango remarked. "It takes a good deal of woodsman's skill, to find your way out of those mountains. That's the trick, you know — the guide disappears as soon as he's got his fee."

By now Brutus was livid. "I'll consider the overtones of all this later," he promised grimly. "Right now we must decide what to do — the ignominious choice of cancelling the performance or switching to some play in which Eric has understudied Ralph. Well, young man, you were about to say something?" He fixed an impatient look upon his son.

With an effort to act casual Eric said, "Just that I've — I've learned Ralph's lines in this one, too."

"You've done what? After I told you to study Snorkey?"

"I've understudied practically everybody," the boy broke out apologetically. "But mostly Ralph. It seemed to me I ought to — I mean, I kept thinking how he — he always was a weak link. He's been an utter fool over gold; I thought he might let us down some time."

Brutus listened with a narrowing look. "You hardly conceived such a notion without suggestion. It's not your nature to be critical. But that's beside the point, right now. How well do you know the part, sir?"

"Letter-perfect," Eric told him eagerly.

"Might say you'd even hoped to do it some day, eh?"

"Well — I — yes, I do like the role. Yes sir."

"And who will fill your own roles? Can you answer me that?"

"We've already got a boy to do Peanuts, and I can still play the signal man in Act Four. The lawyer — "

Eric began to falter under his father's look. "I've been working with one of the supes this last hour, showing him that part. I thought Ralph might — not — be back — in time." His voice faded.

Brutus was nodding angrily. "Very well thought out. So well, in fact, it smacks of too much readiness. Is it possible, young man, that you've been party to some plot?" But Eric was so honestly aghast at the accusation, Brutus relented. His thin lips even twitched slightly as he said, "No, obviously not. Perhaps we should thank Providence that the role tonight calls for an earnest, confused young colt of a hero. A certain natural resemblance exists. I believe I shall try you in it, son. Come now, the rest of you — a hurried supper and be back here by seven."

But Cindy could hardly swallow her food. Slipping away from the others as early as she could, she went back over to the theater, feeling somehow certain that Durango would be there. For now she was sure what was afoot — even how he'd played a part in it.

He was tuning the piano, standing over it with bent head, one hand on the keys, the other on the peg — the one time he'd never let anybody interrupt him, not even Brutus. Cindy grabbed a rag and began to polish the globes on the footlights, working her way closer to him, overflowing with secret knowledge.

When she'd reached a spot right before the piano, he glanced up with a glint of humor. "I thought the lights looked brilliantly clean."

"I bet the piano was in tune, too," she said daringly, for it made her feel like a conspirator, to know she was onto his trick. "You're just trying to keep Brutus away so he won't ask you any more questions right now." Then her voice lowered to a whisper. "You did get that Indian to swipe Ralph, didn't you?"

"How did you come by such an idea?" he hedged, beginning to feel out his octaves again.

"What Eric said, about the utter fool. You told me that too, once. And Eric is the one you meant who had unusual courage, only he's never had a chance to prove it, so — "

"In the matter of courage I had someone else in mind." He glanced at her with an instant of fondness. "Eric was the one on a search — for his own self-respect. If he fails tonight — "

"He won't."

"He could. Eric doesn't know and I don't know. Furthermore, it's not really any of my business. But he kept asking me questions. In between his efforts to justify his presence here, he kept prodding me about what it was like in other places, trying to get the feel of the escape. And Brutus, unaware. It seemed only fair to try to give a father what help I could. I'm beginning to have a sympathy for the problems of fathers."

"Brutus? You're doing this for *him?*"

"He's about to lose the boy. One way or another." Durango struck a strong chord and held it so that the overtones vibrated. "There comes a time when a young man needs to find his own pitch and rhythm. If he doesn't, he'll soon not have much tone of his own. I doubt that Brutus really wants his son to be an echo." He glanced over his shoulder; they could hear the distant sound of voices. And yet Durango went on speaking to her intently, as if it were important she should know his reasons.

"Brutus doesn't even realize how completely he's been dictating every slight expression, each turn of the head. He just knows that Eric is young and uncertain, too retiring by nature to be at ease on his own yet. He wants to help him, that's all. I'm beginning to see that it's hard, for a parent to let an offspring go ahead and make mistakes. And yet it's everybody's priceless right. Of course, whether that justifies me in meddling . . ."

The others were coming now. Cindy whispered, "I'm glad! I'm glad you did. I think old Eric was about to bust, all right. Only I still don't see why you said your future depends on it."

"That's because, when it comes to my skulduggeries" — Durango glanced at her strangely — "you don't know the half of them yet."

23

WHEN CINDY THOUGHT about that performance, afterward, lying in bed some time in the early hours next morning, she kept seeing Eric again — how proud he'd looked. Flushed and a little glassy with excitement, he stood so steady, holding Helene's and Lorna's hands as the curtain came down slowly on the last act, while the audience raised the roof.

They had really taken to Eric. Maybe he lacked Ralph's smooth touch, but his boyish impulsiveness was just right for the role. Time and again the audience burst into applause for him. For them all, really, because the troupe had outdone themselves to help him through. Even Helene played to him more warmly than she ever did with Ralph. And the minute the curtain touched the floor, the whole company crowded around to shake the boy's hand. Then they quieted as Eric turned to look at Brutus.

He stood studying his son with a new curiosity, smiling a little. "A good rendition, my boy. Not perfect, but original — to an astonishing degree. You've thought hard about the role."

"You taught me how important that was, sir," Eric said, with a shyness that hardly hid his pleasure. "If I hadn't learned to put myself into a part by now, there wouldn't be much hope for me as an actor."

"No need to doubt yourself on that score. And almost as important — the whole troupe turned in a superb performance under stress. Ladies and gentlemen, I felt tonight that we were truly a company at last." Brutus looked around at them gravely, deliberately searching out Durango. "And you, my friend, were exceptional as always. You're perhaps the finest musician who ever graced a theatrical production. But you have a wayward humor." His face took on a rueful resignation. "I regret to say, sir, that you are fired."

It had caught them all with a shock, even Cindy, though she could figure it out well enough as they came off-stage. Ralph was sitting glumly in the office, disheveled and muddy and sore. Cindy hoped he'd get fined hundreds of dollars. But it was plain to see he had told Brutus enough to fix the blame on Durango.

The musician paused to say a final word with Eric, that made the boy color up with pride. Then he bowed to the others, told them good-night much as he always did. When Cindy had started to go to him, he gave her a slight shake of the head. And so she had to stand there and watch him leave, alone. As he paused in the door-way, a dark figure against the night outside, she'd felt a keen pang of sympathy. She knew how it felt, to walk off down a street all by yourself with nowhere to go.

She'd even started to follow him, but Maud had caught her arm.

"I wouldn't do it, child. We don't know the whole story here."

But Cindy did know — most of it anyhow. And no matter what else it was that he'd hinted at, she knew it could never turn her against him. After what he'd done for Eric she wanted his help worse than ever.

As she lay still now, with light just breaking across the sky, some premonition had brought her alert. Some sound . . . just the soft creak of a floor board some-where . . . the click of a door latch. Quietly, so as not to disturb the other women, she got out of bed and went to the window — just in time to see Durango step out onto the street below. He was carrying a light trav-eling bag, heading down toward the stage station!

In a rush, Cindy began to dress. She seized the money bag from under her pillow and was racing downstairs, clutching the sack of coins hard. Because if Durango was really stealing off, deserting her, she thought desperately that she'd get on a stagecoach and ride and ride until her money ran out and then maybe just — die.

Down the street she saw a light in the ticket office of the coach line. Picking up her skirts, she ran through the gray hush of dawn. Burst in at the door — straight into Durango's arms.

"I was just on the way back, to see if you were up." He steadied her for an instant. "Hold on, you're trembling. Here, let's sit down." They went over to the deserted waiting room. The ticket agent had gone back to his living quarters behind the office. They were alone.

"You were going to leave," she accused him shakily, sinking down into one of the seats. "You were buying a ticket."

"For you." He handed it to her, a fare to Denver on the ten o'clock stage. "I wanted you to have it before I talked to you. And this, too." From an inner pocket he took an envelope.

Cindy stared at it — her mother's name. Jill Ferris. And an address in Denver. Her mother's name — "*You found her!*"

"She's safe and well. You'll be with her in a matter of hours," he said.

"Somehow you found her — for me!" Cindy's throat got tight and she had to blink back the tears. But even in her bewilderment, she could see that she had disturbed him sharply with her gratitude.

"Cindy, I told you once — I watch out for my own well-being. And your mother is vital to it."

"My mother is . . . ?"

"I'm in love with her." He said it so quietly, with such a warmth, a tenderness in his eyes so strange for Durango — it jolted Cindy out of her confusion.

"In love. With my *mother!*"

"You'll understand some day how it can happen — just with a look. After all those years, I wasn't alone any more." He began to pace the room. "But she wouldn't even let me court her. She was afraid it would hurt you. She doubted that you'd ever accept me — or any man — into your family. I was still trying to convince her, but then the raid caught us. I saw a chance to help, by rescuing you from the Judge. All I ever intended was to get you out of town somehow, and back to her. And yet as I watched for you that night — "

"You were following me!"

"As close as I could. You were doing pretty well at dodging."

"*Why didn't you say so?*"

"Because I suddenly got this idea — to find out whether you and I might just take a shine to each other. We're really two of a kind — I'm leery of most people myself. I've been on the run plenty of times. Even when you were most suspicious of me, I couldn't blame you. It was justified, too — there in Pueblo I was stalling."

"You were lying, about needing a job."

"By then I could see that Jill was right — you'd never take to me unless I could prove myself. I needed time. That's when I got in touch with your mother. She was already with friends of mine in Denver. I had told her where to go, to wait for me there. But I wrote and asked her to give me a few weeks with you."

"All along . . ." Cindy felt as if she were crumpling up inside. "You knew all along . . . where she was."

"Don't look at me like that, Cindy! How else could we have gotten to know each other on even terms? Just you and me — it had to be like that or not at all. Should I have just given up? With my whole happiness hanging in the balance, and maybe yours — "

"I'd have been happy to know my mother was all right!" she burst out violently. "And she must have — didn't she *care?*"

"So much that she gave her consent. To care" — his face toughened — "is to take risks. To play it the hard way. Of course it disturbed her, but she realized, after what happened in Kansas, that she'd been working too hard to get to know you very well. So she trusted me to try my way. I was aware that you'd grieve, but I thought you could stand up to it. You're nearly a woman, grown. All you needed was to get your balance. That's why I figured you should be on your own for a while. At least it's the only way I've ever been able to settle anything — to ask all the hard questions and answer them, myself. That's the other reason I took this chance — I had to find out whether I could handle the problems I might be up against with a family. Not just you — you've got the kind of keenness and gumption that I can understand. But there might be others some day, a son like Eric. He plagued me, that boy!"

Cindy didn't want to think about Eric, but she had to listen to the driving force of the words, as Durango went on, talking to her and to himself as if it were all one.

"Ready to stand on his own feet — almost past the point of readiness. At least I thought so. If I had guessed wrong, it might have ruined his confidence permanently. It could have undone the whole troupe. It would've just about killed Brutus, I think — he's been afraid to try the boy. But if Eric had been my son, that's still how I'd have played it. So if he had failed I'd never again have been able to trust my judgment completely. The greatest risk I ever took — " Then he broke off. "No, there was one greater than that." He came back to stand in front of her squarely, his hands shoved deep in his pockets. "And as for my judgment, the final word is up to you."

Cindy could hardly bear that look, stripped of all defenses, no longer secret and guarded. The blue eyes almost scorched with their demand to know what she might be thinking. He seemed to pry into her mind, to read the hurt there.

"All you need do," he said at last, "is take that envelope — "

"What's in it?" she asked numbly.

"A letter from me to your mother, telling her goodby. I wrote it in case you should decide against me. You know me by now. You know I'd lead you a random kind of life, where questions would have to get explored and answers searched out. Where you'd have to make up your own mind — about a lot of things. Because I'd never mold you. You'd have to do that yourself."

Cindy stared down at the letter, to avoid that steady gaze of his, like a challenge. She had to fight against her own blind impulse to yearn for this man — this man who'd fooled her so —

Durango turned at last and went over to stand at the window. "If you can't forgive me the game I've played, then take that letter, get on the stage — you'll be in Denver by tonight and I'll be so far in the other direction that — "

"No!" It was wrung from her so sharply it brought her to her feet.

Slowly he walked back then, to take her by the shoulders with those strong hands. Only one other person had ever held her that way as if she were something valuable.

"I know," he said softly, "I know how you must feel. But think how high the stakes were, riding on this gamble of mine. Not only a wife, but to win a daughter — " Durango seemed to catch on the word. His face lightened with a look of discovery, a dawning gladness that made Cindy smile, too. And something began to happen, between the two of them . . . something wonderful.

As they stood together at the window of the station, waiting for the stagecoach, Durango kept an arm around her as if she still might somehow escape him. But Cindy's resentment had drained away, and she could fill up with the wonderful thought of seeing her mother again. Most of all, the new prospect — that they wouldn't be alone any more, to have to keep moving along, worrying. There'd be this keen-eyed man looking out for them. Never again would she have to say *who cares?*

Durango was watching up the street now. "Here they come," he said. It was the whole troupe, hurrying down the board sidewalk toward them with Brutus in the lead, his long hair lifting with every stride. "I was hoping they'd come to see us off and wish us well. And I think I can tell them where they can hire another piano player."

"After the way Brutus fired you, I don't even want to say good-by to him," Cindy said, looking around the station. "Can't we hide somewhere and let the ticket-man tell them we've gone?"

Durango shook his head. "I've sworn off lying and tricks. Some member of my family might object to them. Besides, Brutus was absolutely within his rights to deal with me as he did. Don't hold it against him. Because I'm hoping he'll do us a favor. I'd like you to appear in that play again. Just once more — with your mother in the audience."

Such a thought — Cindy was astounded. "Could we?"

"We've got to try to arrange it somehow."

"And with you playing the piano!"

"That's not important. The main thing is you," he told her warmly. "You've always been the best part of the show."

Which meant, of course, that Durango hadn't completely given up fibbing. But Cindy thought — just possibly — this was how it should be, with fathers.